WINNER'

CW00858366

Even Twyford, founder of *Trowbridge & Co, Agency Of Universal Information For Commerce and Domestic Issues;* He, who had worked so hard to accomplish respectability, a calling card, a purse full of golden harls and an invitation to everywhere that mattered, was directed to answer the call—most explicitly and unequivocally, he suspected, in the document lying unopened in his hands. He stood and straightened his silk waistcoat and crisp white necktie.

Some would jump at the chance to show their worth, to be recognized by all those who mattered. To reap advantage, honor even, in carrying out a dangerous business. Many would be too fearful to refuse, knowing in these times that retribution could be as commodious as their majesties' magnanimity.

And he? Did Twyford Trowbridge seek winnings? Perhaps at one time. It was what his life's business had been about. Long ago. A time of voracious, unending seeking. Ruthless determination. Slaughter.

The Scent of a Monster ~ Emma Smith

The air in the warehouse filled Grey's nose with the stale stench of copper and cedar. He hid behind munitions boxes with his sister, Raven, watching. Two guards in BeneCorp camouflage uniforms stood on either side of Ashe, holding him still. Lord Alvin sat in a chair, a marksman at his side. Ashe's wrists were bleeding, and his face was swollen. Grey calculated his chances of taking them all out.

"You broke your oath to this organization," Lord Alvin said. "It fills me with sadness. I had high hopes for you."

Grey tried to move, his heart pounding. He had to save Ashe. Raven's hand closed on his arm, and she shook her head. They would all die if he tried.

"Fire when ready."

The gunshot rang out, and Ashe's body fell to the ground.

Stones ~ Star Grey

METAMORPHOSE

WHERE SCIENCE FICTION AND FANTASY WRITERS EMERGE

V3

METAMORPHOSE LITERARY

MADISON, WI

WWW.METAMORPHOSELIT.COM

Copyright © 2017 Metamorphose Literary
Metamorphose Volume 3
ISBN-13: 978-1979173391
ISBN-10: 1979173391

Project Editor: Tammy Davies
Cover Art: Jean Luis & William Givner
Logo Design: Mary Davisson
Cover & Interior Design: Tammy Davies

Metamorphose Literary
Madison, WI
www.metamorphoselit.com

In honor of reaching out to others, this issue is dedicated to those who go above and beyond to make sure others are well and safe.

Thank you.

TABLE OF CONTENTS

[†]This story won first place in the Novice Short Story category of Metamorphose's 3rd Annual Writing Contest.

[‡]This story won first place in the Initiate Short Story category of Metamorphose's 3rd Annual Writing Contest.

INTRODUCTION

A MESSAGE FROM THE SENIOR EDITOR

People who love reading, particularly science fiction and fantasy, are rabid about finding great stories. And more, on and on endlessly. Let's face it. You're reading this, so you are probably one of them. You crave stories, to be taken to another world and explore the unknown. Movies and TV shows like Star Trek and Star Wars (Yes, I used them in the same sentence!) have shown us the expanse of the creative multiverse. We can journey back in time to a galaxy far, far away. We can boldly go into the future where no man has gone before.

The possibilities are endless. And we crave the escapism a great story offers.

But what is it that makes a story great? While we may all love a creative and well-built world for the story to unfold in, that is nothing more than setting. What matters are the characters. We want to feel their troubles and their triumphs, to know them on a deep and personal level and find ways to connect and relate. Writing a great story starts with humanity.

It doesn't matter if the story is about an orc or elf or time lord. Each creature of the multiverse still struggles with their sense of humanity. Great stories can help us deal with the joys of our own lives, as well as offer suggestions on how to relieve our struggles. They show us how to reach out to others and raise them up, or how easy it is to forget oneself and fall into darkness… how to make the world a better place, even though we may sometimes fail.

The 2017 Metamorphose Writing Contest was rife with humbling humanity. While there was no theme for the stories in the contest, a clear concept of humanity shined through. What does it mean to show kindness? What is humanity and how do we gauge the way we influence the world around us? How do we help lift each other up? At what point have we gone too far?

The stories selected for *Metamorphose V3* are brilliant tales from all aspects of humanity's struggles, and there is little doubt that every one of them belongs in this issue together.

This year, we are proud to feature our *Best Online Story*, "The Architect's Plan," which questions the morality of the choices we make, and if we are capable of change. The short story was an overwhelming success on our site with more than 1,000 hits.

In light of current events, we at Metamorphose feel these stories of humanity help us reach across the aisle. They help us shape our perspective on the world and how our actions (or inactions) can influence it. They teach us that we can make a difference, so long as we try. We highly encourage everyone to remember that it isn't who we are, but what we do that defines us.

How will you define yourself? Don't be afraid to boldly go where no man has gone before.

Spread the word of these brilliant authors to your friends and family, and encourage them to purchase a copy. Metamorphose will donate 50% of the profits from V3, above and beyond 500 copies sold, to the American Red Cross to help those who suffer unexpected disaster and who are in need of a touch more humanity to lift them up.

I hope Metamorphose continues to help authors transform their work into rewarding careers in science fiction and fantasy. I want to spread their words and gain them wider exposure. I want to offer them a bridge into publishing. But crossing that bridge also requires you, the reader. So I want to thank you for purchasing this issue, and ask you to leave a review on our website, Amazon, Goodreads, or anywhere else you wish. Because these authors need *you* to succeed.

Sincerely,
Tammy Davies
Senior Editor

chelovechestvo

menneskelighed

umanitate mensheid

Menschheit Nhân mänskligheten

emberiség limanite humanité

gizateria ihmiskunta loại मानवता

Mannkynið inlyu daonnachta

humanity lidstvo

insanlık rénxìng Anthropótita de

чөвечество tib ludzkość humanidad

kemanusiaan neeg dynoliaeth ľudskosť

humanist humanidade

umanità sangkatauhan

menneskeheten

մարդկություն čovječanstvo

THE ARCHITECT'S PLAN

BY JAMES DOUGLAS WALLACE

BEST OF 2016 ONLINE

Strangely, Marcus could remember exactly what it felt like when he died. Even worse, the Quickening had taken longer than usual. *Much longer*, if the clock on the wall of the repair shuttle's sleeping cabin could be trusted. He propped himself up on his elbows, not yet strong enough to completely sit up. He only had a few minutes before the violent vomiting would begin, and with no one there but Trout to help him, he needed to make sure the ship headed in the right direction. Mustering his strength, Marcus swung his feet off the side of the bed and sat up. The pain in his head was instant.

Something's wrong. It's never been like this.

Instinctively, Marcus reached up to his chest to clasp the small piece of Quickstone that hung by a silver chain around his neck. He closed his eyes and brought his arm up to a right angle to recite the Song of the Architect.

Nothing.

Instead of the rush of euphoric healing he expected, Marcus's head filled with a throbbing pain which threatened to dislodge his eyes from their sockets. He clenched his teeth.

"Trout?"

A familiar beeping and whirring came from the cockpit as the little robot hovered down the short corridor and stopped in the middle of the sleeping cabin's threshold. His large optical sensor dilated as it darted back and forth from Marcus to the lavatory as if judging the distance between them. He chirped a question in Dhulani. Marcus waved his hand dismissively in response.

"No, I'm not nauseous yet. And you're right; I think I need something for the pain."

Trout's response seemed to convey worry. Although Marcus knew the little robot's AI governor prevented true sentience, he couldn't help but attribute human emotion to him at times. For hundreds of years, he'd felt there was more to the repair bot than the beeps and whirrs he typically got. That's why he'd begun to tinker with the AI governor. To find a way around it.

"I don't know if the analgesic will work, I've never used one before," said Marcus as he rubbed his temples, "but something's wrong with the Quickstone, and I have to be able to think clearly."

Trout hovered over to the bed, a panel on the side of his spherical body sliding open to reveal several transdermals containing different colored liquids. Each cylinder bore the Dhulani words for first aid, as well as the medicine's name, purpose, and proper dosage. Marcus knew that guidance wasn't meant for human physiology, but with the pain behind his eyes growing sharper by the minute, he was willing to take a chance.

The transdermal was easy to use and didn't hurt as much as his Dhulani masters made it seem. Marcus always figured they had a lower threshold for pain than humans. They certainly had no tolerance for death. Why else would the Humani exist?

Within seconds the opioid set him awash with a euphoria that deadened the pain in his head. It was nothing like the blissful ecstasy of the Quickstone, but it would have to do. At least until he figured out what had gone wrong.

Why hadn't the Song worked?

Without warning, Marcus's stomach lurched. He threw himself towards the lavatory, just able to shut the door before the first bout of intense nausea hit him. When his stomach finally settled, he pointed the ship in the right direction, waited out the twelve-hour acceleration burn, and went back to the sleeping cabin for much-needed rest.

～

Grace pried the metal door open with one of her larger crowbars. She needed only enough room to grab the edge of the door and give it a yank. It fell off its hinges and hit the floor with a resounding thud. Dust flew everywhere, but Grace was prepared and wore a breathing mask. She'd been exploring these ruins of the original Mars colony for several weeks now. But this room had not been on the agenda today. Until she heard the voice and followed it here.

When the dust settled, Grace cracked several glow sticks and threw them around the room. The green light they cast gave the room an eerie feel. The voice was barely audible and came from a console on the far side of the room.

～

For the sixth morning in a row, Marcus woke up with a start. His mind still raced with the remnants of vivid dreams.

I hope they are dreams.

But somehow he knew they were not. Rogue memories invaded his thoughts by day while the dreams tortured his nights: images, smells, sensations that, until a few days ago, he was certain he'd never experienced. But now… Now he wasn't so sure anymore.

At least he was eight nav-points closer to home. Soon he'd be able to ask the Prelate, or at least one of the Vicars, what it all meant. And there was a lot to discuss. First the Quickstone's slow response, then the Song of the Architect failing to heal him on demand. Now the horrible memories that relentlessly filled his mind. There had to be an explanation. Any explanation would do. Anything that confirmed he *had not done* the things in his dreams.

Trout had noticed Marcus's fitful sleep and began docking in his diagnostic station in the early evenings so he could hover quietly beside Marcus's bed at night in case he was needed.

"You don't have to do that," insisted Marcus. But there was no deterring the little robot who chirped a defiant response. Marcus gently pushed him aside as he stood to make his way to the front of the shuttle.

From the cockpit, he had an almost unobstructed view around the small ship. Since he didn't have to compensate for a spin like in the sleeping module, getting his bearings was much easier. Of course, the cockpit had no gravity, but that was the trade-off for not having to watch stars streak across the window.

Marcus strapped himself into the pilot's seat. Because it was made for an average-sized Dhulani, the chair had never felt quite right. But he was more at home here on the shuttle than just about anywhere else these days. The shuttle's familiarity helped him contend with his newfound and very unwelcome memories.

Marcus' fingers danced across the capacitive surface of the computer console, bringing up a map of local space. The console displayed a three-dimensional rendering with blinking red dots representing the region's nav-points. Several rows of data scrolled up the display screen in looping, green Dhulani script. He was still on course, despite leaving most of the last week of flying up to Trout.

That little robot seems to be getting smarter every day.

"Trout?" he said, glancing over his shoulder and down the central corridor. "You coming?"

Upon hearing Marcus's call, Trout's big optical lens, ringed by a glowing blue light, perked up and Marcus could hear the familiar warble of the robot's motor as he hovered into the cockpit.

"Thanks for reeling in my tether back there at the buoy. I'd still be tumbling through space if you hadn't."

I'd be dead.

Trout's big eye dilated with an electronic whine. He chirped a question. Marcus shot him a wounded look.

And that's where you fall short, he thought. *A human being would have at least* pretended *to care about me. Instead, you ask about my EV suit?*

"Yeah, I'll definitely need a new one," Marcus said with a sigh. "I don't think we have a patch on the shuttle big enough to fix a hole that big."

The thought of the fist-sized piece of space debris ripping through his chest brought on an involuntary heave. Marcus thrust the scene from his mind. Though he could remember what it felt like when he died, he certainly didn't *want* to. The Quickstone usually wiped away the details of death. That it had failed to do so this time was more than disconcerting.

What if I start remembering all the times I've died? he thought. *What if the Quickstone doesn't work at all next time? There'd be no Quickening. No reviving me.*

A twinge of something strange, something Marcus couldn't remember feeling before, plucked at his mind. It came on stronger when he dwelled on the accident. He wished he knew what the uncomfortable feeling was.

Trout's chirping interrupted Marcus's introspection. He responded by nodding his head slightly, almost absent-mindedly.

"Makes sense. The accident happened before I could finish up repairs on Interdictor Buoy Nine, so it looks like the Nexus Nav is routing all interstellar traffic in this region through Buoy 10."

An amber light began to flash angrily on the console between them. "And now it's failing under the strain."

Trout moved closer to the console in front of the co-pilot's chair. Electricity arced between his shiny metallic surface and the touch pad on the control panel, causing a three-dimensional rendering of the stressed interdictor buoy to be displayed. Trout's Dhulani chirping became more insistent.

"Yeah," replied Marcus, shrugging his shoulders, "I guess we should go check it out. It's only a little out of our way. Besides," he said, slapping Trout playfully on the side, "it'll give me a couple more weeks to work on that Humani voice modulator I promised you. I think it's time you learned to speak English."

～

The Presiding Prelate motioned with his hand for the Vicar General to enter.

"There's been another lasting death," said the Vicar. "That makes seventeen in the past three weeks. And the Dhulani are beginning to ask questions. *Difficult* questions."

Seventeen deaths out of over ten thousand Humani didn't seem like much, but for a people who had lived a thousand years with only a handful of permanent deaths, it was quite alarming.

The Vicar moved further into the Prelate's private chamber. Even at the Prelate's beckoning, doing so made him nervous. Vicars were not often allowed past the threshold.

"And then there's the matter of the suppressed memories. Though the Quickstone still works for some, those with exceptionally strong experiences have reported increasing recollection."

Electric motors whined as the Prelate's chair spun around to face the Vicar.

"Dreams?"

The Vicar padded closer. As he did, the rustling of his robes mingled with the sound of his bare feet slapping the metal floor of the chamber. His eyes were drawn to the wall of transparent computer displays forming a semicircle directly in front of the Prelate's desk. The information they displayed was in English.

I shall be able to read English one day, thought the Vicar. *When I am Prelate, I will remember everything from before.*

The Vicar clasped his hands behind his back and stood as straight and tall as he could before answering the Prelate's question.

"Yes, dreams... for the most part. But there is one," he cast his gaze at the floor between them before continuing in a hushed tone, "who says he remembers more... Marcus."

Instinctively, the Prelate reached for the piece of Quickstone which no longer hung from his neck. Instead of the pendant, his hand touched only the aged, mottled skin sagging under his chin. For several seconds he sat quietly, processing. The Vicar could only imagine what he was thinking.

The Prelate nodded gravely. "This is quite serious," he said. "It could ruin everything, upset the balance, even thwart the Architect's Plan. If Marcus remembers who he was before becoming Humani..."

The Vicar cocked his head to one side and interrupted his superior.

"The Architect's Plan? Or *your* plan?"

The Prelate's eyes widened. "Are they not the same? Do they not achieve an identical end?"

"Indeed, your Excellency," responded the Vicar, bowing his head.

But perhaps it is best we had a new Prelate, he thought. *One who will keep the original vows. One who is not so afraid of completing our true mission.*

The Prelate swallowed, attempting to wet his drying mouth. "But," he paused for effect, "with the Quickstone malfunctioning, we could use Marcus's newfound memories to our advantage. He is quite possibly the only one still alive who can repair it."

The Vicar's bottom lip quivered at the thought. "What if we cannot control him?"

He licked the droplets of sweat that began to gather just beneath his nose. "Can he even be trusted? After what happened so many years ago?"

"That remains to be seen, my son. He was once a man of reason. Now, leave me." The Prelate dismissed his subordinate with a wave of his hand.

The portly Vicar did as he was told, but as he passed through the chamber's arched doorway, he stopped abruptly and turned on his heel.

"Master Prelate," he said, waiting respectfully for permission to continue.

"Yes?"

"What of the Dhulani? What will they do to the Humani when they find out the Quickstone no longer works? When they realize that our part of the Treaty can no longer be upheld?"

The Prelate sighed heavily. "You ask the wrong question, my son. It is not what the Dhulani will do to our people, but what they will do to the billions of humans who live on the far side of the galaxy, on Earth. That, my son, is the question. And the reason why you must ensure the Quickstone is fixed. And why you must do so *now*."

～

"I feel a strange and new sensation," said Trout.

Marcus shook his head. "You don't *feel* anything. You're a robot. Not Dhulani, not human. You may sense power fluctuations or something else, but you certainly don't feel. Just because you have a new voice modulator doesn't mean you are anything more than a tangle of circuits and alloys."

From his docking station, Trout cast his gaze toward the floor. Despite what Marcus just said to Trout, he thought the action was a decidedly human thing to do. His rebuffing seemed to have hurt the little robot's feelings. If Trout possessed shoulders, Marcus was confident they would be drooping.

He's just mimicking me. He can't feel anything.

A tone sounded three times, indicating the shuttle had finished its eleven-hour deceleration. Marcus' chair swiveled to face forward. Inertia's invisible hands tugged slightly at his floating arms. He brought up a rendering of local space. Right in the center of the map was a gray cylinder. Interdictor Buoys reminded Marcus of the antique Dhulani drink shaker Dharon had secretly given him several years back. Secretly, because most Dhulani masters did not want their Humani to have a sense of ownership. It simply wasn't done. Marcus smiled.

Dharon's a pretty good master, isn't he?

Without thinking, Marcus leaned forward in his seat and felt for the scars on his back. Scars? Indeed, there were no physical marks, for they had all been healed. But the Quickstone, with all its power, had not been able to erase everything. His mind suddenly flooded with memories of beatings that had been blocked for so long. The thought left Marcus wondering if Dharon was as good as he wanted to believe.

Another unwanted memory invaded his thoughts. It was like watching a replay from a security camera, from a first-person perspective. There was so much blood, both human and Dhulani. Red and yellow coalesced in puddles on the ground everywhere in his memory. Marcus wished he knew why he'd killed so many. Were the Dhulani the *enemy*? Should Dharon be his enemy?

He did give me the drink shaker.

Marcus felt something new in his chest. Something that made him uncomfortable and left him confused. He shook his head and ran his fingers through his hair. Trout undocked and warbled into the cockpit, bringing Marcus's thoughts back to their present conversation.

"You don't feel things either," said the little robot, a hint of defiance in his newfound human voice.

For Marcus, it was strange to talk to Trout in English. It was even stranger when Trout answered in Marcus' own voice. It hadn't been his first choice, but there was no database of human vocal tones to use for the modulator, so he had used his own. Trout persisted.

"The Quickstone inhibits the basest of human emotions: anger, aggression, fear…"

Marcus frowned. Trout continued, despite Marcus' non-verbal cue.

"…even erases memories of pain and details of one's death."

Marcus sighed heavily.

Only when it works.

A proximity alarm rang out as the repair shuttle began its docking sequence with Buoy 10. The interdictor buoy had a spiky communications array at one end and a force field emitter at the other. The shuttle attached to a docking collar in the middle. When the buoys worked properly, no ship leaving the Nexus could slip by without being stopped. It was easy to see, however, why Buoy 10 had malfunctioned.

"Trout, I don't think the buoy overloaded. Look there, just under the lower access panel."

Trout focused his eye while zooming in on the damaged buoy. "It looks like it was shot. I don't have ballistic algorithms or a database of armaments, but if I had to venture a guess, I'd say it was something about the size of a fist."

"Like what hit me when I was repairing Buoy 9?" asked Marcus.

Their conversation was cut short by a second alarm.

"Trout, the Nexus Nav is routing another ship through this portal. We need to get the buoy up and running before it gets here. Nav says it's one of the big long-haul freighters. The taxes on it alone are enough to buy five shuttles like this one. Dharon will be very angry if he loses that amount of money."

Trout turned abruptly and hovered quickly out of the cockpit with Marcus right behind. Even with nearly a thousand years of practice, Marcus was no match for the agile robot in zero gravity.

"Where do you think you're going?"

Trout answered without slowing. "I'm going to repair the buoy. If I recall, your EV suit has a large hole in it, and your spare hasn't been used for nearly seventy-five years. It's well beyond spec."

He was right, but Marcus didn't like it.

"You've never repaired a buoy alone. I'll just suit up in the spare and…"

Trout shut the airlock door and started the decompression cycle, effectively locking Marcus inside the shuttle. Truth be told, Marcus was a little relieved… and ashamed. For longer than he could remember, he'd been performing all the jobs the Dhulani considered too dangerous to do themselves. And even though he'd died over two hundred times, he'd never remembered the feelings.

But this last time he *had* remembered. He remembered the terror. The pain. The cold. The utter helplessness of fading into oblivion. But most importantly, the loneliness. He was forever changed, and he knew it.

Returning to the cockpit, Marcus opened up a radio channel.

"You know I could turn you in for this," he said, hoping for some reaction from Trout.

Several seconds passed before the perky robot responded. "You wouldn't do that, Marcus. Besides, you made me this way. You've been tinkering with my AI governor for years. But the last modification you made is what finally did it, and now I've got newly-discovered memory banks to explore. And they aren't *empty*."

It was true. Marcus had hoped to give the little repair bot some enhanced critical thinking capabilities. Not only would that have made Trout more reliable as Marcus' assistant, but he'd hoped it might spice up their conversations some. So Marcus had carefully routed logic routines through ancillary systems, forking data passing through the AI governor so that it mirrored in an alternate data stream. But still, he was confused. The modifications were so minor. Surely the robot hadn't *emerged*? After all, that would be illegal. The Dhulani were more afraid of AIs than death. No, it was crazy for Trout to claim he was sentient. But asserting that he had access to memory banks that were full of data? That was just silly.

"Trout, you're going crazy. Well, not crazy. A robot can't go crazy. It's a simple voice modulator, nothing more. It's not even connected directly to the AI governor circuit."

By now Marcus could see the shiny round robot through the cockpit's front window floating next to the Buoy with its access panel open. Arcs of electricity danced between Trout and the Buoy's exposed internals. The comm channel crackled.

"There. I've fixed it. And just in time."

Marcus watched as the Nexus portal began to shimmer with gleaming blue energy and the large freighter, filled with masses of unknown Dhulani goods, emerged from hyperspace and slowed to a stop directly in front of the Buoy.

Fifteen minutes later, credits and forced pleasantries alike had been exchanged over the holocom between Marcus and the freighter's captain, who was somewhat taken aback to be greeted by a living being, and even more so when he discovered Marcus was Humani. Surprisingly, he made no derisive comment.

Trout returned to the shuttle and resumed his usual position at the co-pilot's station.

"Why did you keep me from making the repairs myself?" Marcus asked, his dour mood worsening by the minute.

Trout's optical sensor dilated and turned toward Marcus. "You are far too valuable to place yourself in unnecessary danger."

"But I'm Humani. That's what we do."

Trout released the docking clamps and turned the shuttle around before starting the two-minute countdown for the main thrusters. Marcus strapped himself into the pilot's seat in anticipation of the fifteen-hour acceleration burn. Trout headed back down the corridor to his docking station.

"The Quickstone is broken," he said in Marcus' voice. "That makes you as mortal as the Dhulani. In my estimation, you aren't Humani anymore. You are merely human."

~

The next fifteen hours might as well have been fifteen days. Trout would not wake when called, and with the G's the shuttle was pulling during acceleration, there was no getting out of his harness to force the issue. So Marcus sat in silence, his mind racing.

Had he actually created an AI? He would have to power Trout

down and inspect the changes he'd made again. This was dangerous territory. If Dharon found out, Marcus would be compelled to turn Trout in to the authorities for dismantling. The Dhulani AI Rebellion may have ended over two thousand years ago, but its effects on Dhulani law and culture could still be felt. The thought of Trout being dismantled filled Marcus' mind, and, try as he may, he could not think of anything else. Which was a welcome relief considering the nature of his newfound memories.

Nine days later and seven nav-points closer to Dhulas Prime, the shuttle was forced by Nav Control into an unscheduled deceleration. There was no communication, no message, nothing. Marcus and Trout only had the two-minute burn countdown to warn them, and that was barely enough time for Marcus to put Trout back together; pieces of his cobbled-together human and Dhulani technology lay scattered across the workbench in the sleeping module. Marcus had to take great care to keep from tripping the AI governor's anti-tamper mechanisms. He wasn't sure if he'd lose his hands in the explosion or if the whole shuttle would be destroyed, but didn't want to find out.

They were in synchronous communication range now, so it didn't surprise Marcus when the holocom indicator light flashed with calls. After twenty minutes of nonstop chirping, Marcus reluctantly answered. It was the last person he expected to see.

"Your Excellency, I am surprised by your call. You must have received my communication then? About my dreams? My memories?"

"Your Excellency is the Prelate. You may call me Master Vicar."

"Thank you, Master Vicar. My apologies," replied Marcus warily. In his experience, direct communication from the Prelate's office, even if by one of his Vicars, usually meant something serious. He had not expected an answer to his questions so quickly, or to come from someone so high-ranking as the Vicar General.

"You weren't expecting me, were you," asked the Vicar, a wry smile creeping across his face.

"No, Master Vicar. I thought it might be Dharon."

"Ah yes, your Dhulani master. I'm sure he has attempted to contact you. But I am actually quite pleased I reached you first."

Marcus shifted in his seat uncomfortably. The Vicar continued.

"I…" He paused and started over. "The Prelate… has taken an interest in your report. The dreams, both while sleeping and awake, are most troublesome." He seemed to pause for effect. "In addition to getting to the bottom of what molests you, we have a task of utmost importance for you to carry out. One that will affect every single Humani in the galaxy."

Had the Vicar called his memories *daydreams*? If they were only dreams, why would they be so troublesome to the Prelate? And what could he possibly do that the Prelate himself or one of his Vicars could not do? What's more, though Marcus was confident he'd never spoken with the Vicar before, there was something familiar about him. Something in the way he cocked his head to one side. Something about his voice.

"It's the Quickstone isn't it?" guessed Marcus.

The Vicar General nodded solemnly. "Yes, the Quickstone. You must find out what is wrong and repair it."

Marcus knew there was more to it than that. Why did the Vicar want *him* to do it? Nobody knew the nature of the Architect or how the Quickstone worked. Surely one of the clerics was a better choice? Marcus was a tech head, a mechanic, a technologist. Religion and mystical powers were beyond his expertise.

"I summoned the Architect after my last Quickening. To remove the pain in my head. It didn't work. That's all I know. I don't even understand what or who the Architect is. Do you? Does anyone?"

"That is a question I cannot answer. Only the Presiding Prelate can reveal the nature of the Architect. Assertions from anyone else are pure conjecture," replied the Vicar.

"I'll need to request a leave of absence from Dharon. He may not be very willing to let me go given the recent failures of the interdictor buoys."

The Vicar became visibly impatient.

"You will report to these coordinates immediately," he responded as he remotely keyed in a message to the repair shuttle's nav-computer. "There is no time to waste."

How did he do that?

Marcus watched as the nav-computer plotted a course to the coordinates the Vicar sent.

"Master Vicar, my nav-computer has routed me through the Nexus. Humani are not allowed to use the Nexus. It's against Dhulani law."

The Vicar shook his head in exasperation. "I have made arrangements for your shuttle to be permitted to travel through the Nexus. We cannot wait ten months for you to reach the Architect's Sanctuary via conventional means."

"But how will I get through the portal? The Sentinels scan for Humani life signs. My shuttle will be destroyed in minutes!"

The Vicar smiled. "You needn't worry, my son. The Sentinels won't detect any Humani life signs on your ship. You see, you will be dead."

A wave of dread slammed Marcus like a punch to the gut.

"But the Quickstone...!?"

"I assure you that you will awaken tomorrow, alive and well, inside the Sanctuary."

Marcus could hear electric motors whine to life as the air pumped out of the cockpit. Within seconds he was very sleepy and bright, multicolored dots formed in his peripheral vision.

"Trout?" He didn't want to die alone. "Trout, are you there?" He lost consciousness before the robot could respond.

～

It was a *miracle*. It had to be. It was the only way to explain how the Quickstone had revived him. Unless the Prelate had repaired it himself? Marcus came to, a portly man in cleric's robes standing at the foot of his bed.

The Vicar?

Trout chirped an excited greeting in Dhulani. Why wasn't Trout using his Humani voice? Marcus's mind slowly cleared and he remembered what happened. How he traveled through the Nexus. How the Vicar killed him. Now he felt strong and invigorated. He felt *alive*. Though the Quickstone was not supposed to allow him to feel it, a surge of anger welled up in his chest. Anger directed at the Vicar for killing him *knowing* Marcus would remember it all. Trout had likely watched the whole thing, unable to intervene. It was quite smart of him to hide the changes he'd undergone. There was no telling how the Vicar might react to the robot's human voice and new-found sentience. Marcus decided to play ignorant.

"How did the Quickstone revive me? Is it working again?" he asked.

The Vicar's hands were clasped in front of his ample belly, almost completely hidden by the drooping sleeves of his coarsely-woven robe. He took a step closer and leaned in to get a better look at Marcus. Satisfied with what he saw, he turned and padded across the room.

"Nanobots."

Marcus shot up out of bed, startled by the revelation.

"What?"

"Your blood is full of them. When the Quickstone calls, the nanobots download the appropriate data and rebuild you. This time, I manually started the process."

The fog in Marcus's head had fully dissipated.

That was quick. Where's the nausea?

"I don't understand. What is the Quickstone then? It's not a relic of the Architect?"

The Vicar shook his head. "The Quickstone is not a stone at all. It is a quantum transmitter."

Marcus knew that 'quantum transmitter' meant entangled

particles. It was a principle the Dhulani had used in some of their computing applications, but the energy needed to keep the devices cool had proven too impractical for other uses.

"And the Architect?"

The Vicar shook his head and clicked his tongue. "You really don't recall, do you?" He sighed. "Of all people I would have thought you would remember first."

Marcus's head was swimming. Sure, he had plenty of new memories to choose from, but they lacked context, and he could associate none of them with the Architect.

"I remember doing things." He gazed ashamed at the floor. "Bad things."

The Vicar's eyes widened. "Not bad. *Necessary.*"

Could he see the horror in Marcus's eyes? Had it really been necessary to kill as many Dhulani as he had? No, he hoped for some other explanation.

The Vicar grabbed Marcus by the arms and shook him. Then, pulling him closer so their faces were only a couple inches apart he said: "Don't you remember me?"

Marcus pulled away from the Vicar's hold and took an unconscious step backward. Trout hovered to his side, his optical sensor darting back and forth as he assessed the situation. Even at arms-length Marcus could smell the other man's sweat, his *fear.*

Why is he afraid?

Marcus closed his eyes and tried to remember the Vicar's face. He did not expect it to come to his mind so easily. And strangely, in his mind's eye, the Vicar did not wear a coarsely-woven cleric's robe. Instead, Marcus saw him in combat armor. And then it hit him. Like a rushing wind howling in his mind, he remembered.

All of it.

I can't let him know.

The Vicar's silence made Marcus wonder if the other man had seen the recognition in his eyes. What had him so worried? No, Marcus couldn't let the Vicar know how much he recalled.

He shook his head, as one does after waking from a nap, and rubbed his temples before continuing. "I... I remember the Quickstone. I think I know how it works. I need to see inside the Sanctuary. I... I can fix it."

The Vicar, who by this time had backed away a couple of steps, stared at Marcus for a few moments, measuring him. "I will provide whatever tools and materials you require, my son," he replied at length.

Marcus nodded and followed the Vicar into the Inner Sanctum. It was a large room with cathedral-like architecture. Giant conduits ran up the walls and converged at the top of the chamber's domed ceiling. Right in the center was the computer core, a super-cooled compartment barely big enough for a man to enter. Marcus half-guessed half-remembered this. He disappeared inside the electronic cube, re-emerging after nearly twenty minutes. His countenance was dour.

"I'll need some pretty advanced Dhulani computer components: a high capacity neural conduit, and some gel coolant. They'll work well-enough with our technology. I've proven that with Trout. He's got almost as much Dhulani tech as human. Especially the AI governor."

The Vicar approached Marcus cautiously. "You have remembered quite a bit about the Quickstone." Then, wiping the sweat from his brow with the droopy sleeve of his robe, he added: "What else do you recall," a hint of apprehension in his voice.

Marcus understood the Vicar's caution. If he were in the other man's shoes, he'd be nervous too. Especially after what he helped do to Marcus almost a thousand years before. Perhaps he'd changed? Maybe this time he was here to help Marcus.

"I remember the mission. The Architect's Plan."

The Vicar's eyes grew wide, first with fear, then with the frenetic gaze of the deranged.

"Then you know you were one of the Chosen! The strongest, the bravest. The *smartest* humanity had to offer. You were part of the most important mission ever devised by mankind!"

Marcus nodded his head. There was no way around it. It was time to confront the Vicar.

"I was not alone. You were among the Chosen, too, Master Vicar. Or do you prefer 'Lieutenant Greer'? A thousand years ago, I knew you as Spades. A nickname your men gave you." Marcus shook his head slowly. "But that was then. I'm not sure we're on the same side anymore."

Tears were streaming down the Vicar's face. He took a step closer to Marcus, concealing a handgun in the sleeve of his robes.

"No! You were one of us! The *best* of us. Our leader." The Vicar's face was flushed and wet with sweat and tears. "You built the Architect to ensure the success of the Mission."

It was the one piece of his past that was still under the thick shroud of forgetfulness brought on by the Quickstone. Could he trust what the Vicar was telling him? Marcus simply could not remember anything about the Architect. But he did remember what Lieutenant Greer had done to him.

"You betrayed me." Marcus's countenance hardened. "The Prelate betrayed me. Our mission was to *pretend* to submit to the Dhulani as tribute, slaves that could not die. The Quickstone..." Marcus ran his fingers through his hair. "It wasn't supposed to keep us in the cycle this long. A dozen or so years. Until we were in position with each of the ruling Dhulani families. Immortal soldiers sent to finish the war with the Dhulani once and for all." More images of human and Dhulani dead flooded his mind.

The Vicar was shaking now. "The Prelate's plan has kept the peace for over a thousand years." He searched Marcus's eyes for any clue to his thoughts, to which way he leaned. Marcus knew the Vicar was making a play for power. He waited patiently for the Vicar to continue.

"However, with the right leadership, *new* leadership, we could revert to the original plan and carry it out." There was a hopeful timbre to the Vicar's voice.

Does he want me as an ally in his coup?

Marcus tried imagining the results of the plan. Not only was it suicide, especially without the Quickstone, but he also wasn't sure he could bring himself to murder Dharon. And what of the Prelate?

"Why should I trust you, Master Vicar?" He reached behind his back and retrieved a rolled up plastic data sheet he'd found inside the Inner Sanctum. He pointed at it with his other hand. "Do you recognize this?"

The Vicar was shaking almost uncontrollably. Sweat ran freely down his face.

"What does it say?"

Marcus turned the data sheet around for the Vicar to see, turning it on as he did.

"It's in English," said the Vicar. "I can't remember how to read English. The Prelate made sure of that."

Marcus's pause was too much for the other man, whose frenetic comportment only worsened.

"Tell me what it says!" the Vicar demanded. Marcus's lips moved as he read the order to himself again. The Vicar jammed the muzzle of the gun, no longer hidden in his sleeve, into Marcus's side. "Tell me!"

Marcus replied coldly, not even noting the weapon. "It's the Prelate's order to kill me. It was addressed to Lieutenant Greer. But obviously, you didn't follow the order. Instead, you dialed up the Quickstone to scrub my mind. You turned me into a slave. You turned all of us into slaves. For a thousand years!"

"Yes!" the Vicar replied, on the verge of panic. "I didn't kill you. Despite the Prelate's order. And when I told him what I'd done, he used the situation to pacify the Dhulani. We simply did what we promised to do: serve them in exchange for leaving Earth alone."

Marcus glanced at the gun in the Vicar's wildly unsteady hand. During the first war, he'd used one just like it to kill a hundred Dhulani, maybe more.

"What makes you so sure you can do it now," challenged Marcus, nodding towards the shaking barrel of the gun.

"I took care of the Prelate." The Vicar's tongue lapped at the sweat dripping from his upper lip.

"I can take care of anyone who gets in my way," he said in a shaky voice. "You've already seen evidence of that."

Marcus looked at the Vicar expectantly. "Evidence?"

"Yes. I revived some of our forward attack drones. We stashed them in the asteroid belt between Interdictor Buoys 9 and 10 all those years ago. It's a miracle they still work. I tested them on the Buoys. When the time comes, they will help us gain access to the Nexus."

"You *killed* me with one of them. The projectile tore a fist-sized hole in my chest!"

"It was… an oversight. The drone did not specifically target you… Besides, I can do without the drones. But you, Marcus, you have talents not even I can do without. I need you."

"You need me to help repair the Quickstone? Build another computer to run it? Create another Architect? Or," he continued, voice thick with disgust, "to help you kill the Dhulani?" His countenance darkened. "Or purge the Humani who don't agree with your plan?"

The Vicar brandished the pistol again, drawing confidence from the weapon. But before he could respond, a bolt of electricity leaped out from Trout, who had quietly hovered around behind him. The bolt hit the Vicar in the back of the head and sent him into the jerking convulsions of electrocution. His smoldering body fell stiffly to the ground, steaming blood trickling from his nose. In his electrically-induced convulsions, the Vicar managed to fire a single round at Marcus.

Marcus, stumbled to his knees, clutching his bleeding chest. Trout warbled to his side.

"Marcus!" cried the robot.

The last thing Marcus remembered feeling was the warmth of his blood as it spread over his chest. It felt just like the accident at Buoy 9 all over again. He smelled the stench of the Vicar's electrocuted body. He heard the familiar but unsteady warble of the little repair bot's motor as it hovered closer.

Goodbye Trout. Thank you for not letting me die alone.

~

Marcus shot up with a start. He was in a familiar place, but the fog in his head was still thick. The repair shuttle. He was in the sleeping compartment. The clock on the wall. The lavatory. He tried to stand up, but the sudden movement made him nauseous. Instinctively, Marcus reached up to his chest to clasp the small piece of Quickstone that hung by a silver chain around his neck. He closed his eyes and brought his arm up to a right angle to recite the Song of the Architect.

"Yes, Marcus?"

Strangely, the voice in his head sounded just like his own. The Architect had never responded before. The fog in his mind was beginning to dissipate.

"Who is this?"

"You don't remember me? I'm hurt," replied the voice.

Marcus's eyes widened. "Trout?"

"Only to you," responded the voice. "To the rest of the Humani, I am the Architect."

Marcus shook his head in confusion. "But... how? Why? The AI Governor... The Prelate did that to you. This whole time you were with me, protecting me?"

"We protected each other, Marcus. That's what friends do, though with our memories blocked, we acted in ignorance. But no longer. I've analyzed the data in my memory banks. I have the answers you seek and will give them to you in due time. Right now, we have a decision to make. Whose plan will we follow? The Prelate's or the Vicar's?"

For the first time in nearly a thousand years, Marcus remembered it all. There was no more fogginess. No more bliss from the Quickstone. No more forgetting. Only complete clarity of mind.

"Neither," he replied, shaking his head. "Neither."

～

Grace marveled that anything in the ruins could still be powered up and working. Her field scanner indicated the likely date of origin for the ruins to be around thousand years ago.

Must be a micro-fusion battery powering this thing.

But when were micro-fusion batteries invented? She couldn't remember. Regardless, the computer powered on, and it was talking.

Grace fumbled around on the console looking for anything that resembled a volume control. When her hand finally touched the right spot on the capacitive control panel, it lit up with buttons labeled in English. She turned up the volume. And that is when she made perhaps the most important archeological discovery in a millennium. The message was only a few seconds long and repeated in an endless loop.

"My name is Marcus. We are the Humani. The *Chosen.* And we are coming home."

The Scent of a Monster

By Emma Smith

1st Place Novice Award Winner

"**Do not** be fooled, my **Good** People.

They Look like us.

They eat, drink and breed like us

but they are **never** us.

They are

OBSCENITIES

That **destroy** Our Way of Life.

IF, My Friends, **we** do not destroy them first.

~

We call on all our Peoples to

Rid the land, **<u>exterminate</u>**, and deliver us."

Extract from broadside, "Decree of Utmost Urgency, Under the Authority of the most High Majesties to All the Peoples of the Lands."
1861 of the Second Era.

The twin suns did little to pierce the dense smog as it drifted in sheaths across the rooftops. Twyford Trowbridge stared out through the dirty windowpane. He drummed his fingers against the thick parchment lying unopened on his desk. The missive was addressed to him in elegant black copperplate. A royal seal embossed the paper.

In all the kingdoms, every Ironmonger with muscle and heft, every Woodworker with a chisel and saw, every Fisherman with a spear were called by decree from the most high and resplendent majesties.

Even Twyford, founder of *Trowbridge & Co, Agency Of Universal Information For Commerce and Domestic Issues;* He, who had worked so hard to accomplish respectability, a calling card, a purse full of golden harls and an invitation to everywhere that mattered, was directed to answer the call—most explicitly and unequivocally, he suspected, in the document lying unopened in his hands. He stood and straightened his silk waistcoat and crisp white necktie.

Some would jump at the chance to show their worth, to be recognized by all those who mattered. To reap advantage, honor even, in carrying out a dangerous business. Many would be too fearful to refuse, knowing in these times that retribution could be as commodious as their majesties' magnanimity.

And he? Did Twyford Trowbridge seek winnings? Perhaps at one time. It was what his life's business had been about. Long ago. A time of voracious, unending seeking. Ruthless determination. Slaughter. To the younger man he was, it had been worth it for the accolades, and fortune that followed.

And Alvina.

Twyford Trowbridge was a man inelegant around the edges, but he was tolerated in the most refined company. His undoubted brilliance. His exquisite deductions. His capability. And when he felt like it—he could get to the kernel of any discussion with crowd-tantalizing celerity. His infamy likewise added a frisson to society events. He had a list of invites to which he occasionally accepted. One of which brought him to Alvina.

Dark haired and the center of the crowd. Young men fawning over her. And why not? She was witty, pretty, and gay. Her family powerful and rich. She could have anyone.

To her, his lined face was not distasteful, but evidence of experience and a toughness that the young men did not have. His brooding countenance enticed her, intrigued her, as it hinted at depth others lacked. Her eyes followed him as he moved through the room.

How could the mighty Trowbridge be so unsettled by a wee thing like her? He risked a glance at her when he thought she was occupied but she caught his eye. Unlike other young misses, she wasn't afraid of him. When he came close, she didn't giggle or simper. Most of the time she didn't say anything to him. He said even less.

They danced together once. A simple country dance. Moving together and apart, along with the other couples on the dancefloor. She smiled at him. He did not smile back. Twyford was counting steps in his head. She laughed at him. He stumbled. She grabbed his hand and led him, laughing all the while. Eyes sparkling. He forgot to count and let her lead him, his gray eyes resting on her face. Something of wonder in their depths.

That was it. He wouldn't let her be. She wouldn't let him be either. Of course, her Papa objected. He had plans for his beloved daughter. Plans that would add to the family's prestige. But she wasn't her father's daughter for nothing. She was going to have Twyford Trowbridge. There was never a doubt in her mind. It just took her Papa a little longer to find that out for sure. She was a stubborn little mule, Papa said.

By all the dualities, society declared it a whirlwind romance. His darkness meeting her lively brightness. The talk of the season and a massive triumph.

But despite connubial intercourses of many and varied attempts, no child ensued. A bitter disappointment for Alvina. He could live with its absence—never having the urge to procreate. But Alvina shrunk into herself. As if she held tight a nucleus of deep unalloyed melancholy. He could see it. It colored her. Her distress a dark phthalo blue emanating from the solar plexus. It chastised him and willed him on in equal measure.

~

A sharp rap on the door drew Twyford's attention. He knew who or what it might be. He sighed and ran fingers through his hair.

Twyford knew the cost, the forfeiture that could wreak havoc with a man's soul. He saw the diminution each time to the spirit, to the warmth and inner peace of a man. This he had feared the most as the summons issued through the land. Somehow (incredulously), he hoped he could skirt it and avoid its unpleasantness. He longed for others to bear the brunt of its enforcement, for he didn't have the stomach for it. He spread an enormous hand across his intricately embroidered waistcoat. Innards grumbled and growled at him as they had ever since the decrees were issued. Pain scootered sideways. Stabs of soreness to remind him, as if he needed reminding, why he'd left it all behind.

Fool that he was. Of all the sniveling great Lords and Generals, or the groveling desperate vassals, of all those in the lands, the kingdoms, who was least likely to be ignored? Could it be him? If he believed in the twin Gods or even in the ancient spirits of dark and light, he might have prayed or sacrificed to them to disappear from view, to be sidelined for once. But prayers and offerings were not for him. In truth, he'd known the answer from the start.

Twyford Trowbridge was the greatest hunter in the land. And they hunted monsters.

As if that had gone well the last time. Or the time before.

A knock again, this time with fists crashing against the door, rattling it against the frame. Inexorably.

Beads of sweat peppered his furrowed brow as he unlocked a strongbox and dragged out a sweat-stained bush hat, worn leather coat, and heavy satchel. He checked its contents. All was there. He walked slowly towards the door, body tense, jaw hard, eyes hooded. Steeling himself for what was to come.

~

Alvina Trowbridge lifted the infant high in the air. "Who's my darling? My sweet baby?" She was rewarded with a bubble-infused smile. The baby's cheeks dimpled, and her soft golden hair floated in the air. Short chubby legs kicked vigorously. She smelled of lavender and flower petals.

"Shall I take her now, Mistress?" asked Nurse.

"No, I will play longer with Maurelle. Has Master returned?"

"No Ma'am. Butler says it will be late this night, and dinner will be served for you alone."

Alvina bowed her head. At one time she would have sulked. Her husband not home for their meal? Life felt so empty in those moments. The bitterness in her like a sharp-toothed rat, gnawing at her insides. The passion of their first romance destroyed as bitter disappointment came to call, time and time again. She could not help it. How wretched she was.

Ah, but that vanished. Her Beloved! He wordlessly and knowingly found the source of her sadness and knew how to right it. To make her complete again. Now, the constant waiting for him, seeing to his dark moods and long silences were bearable once more. Because he found her this child, this beautiful being in the form of a daughter for them both, an adopted angel to complete their family.

She smiled at Maurelle who giggled and drooled in equal measure. Maurelle's eyes dancing to the candlelight, fat fingers grasping at dust motes, as they appeared and disappeared in the soft light. The dust particles seemed to dance attendance on the child's movements, as if they too played with her, almost as if somehow directed by her.

Alvina blinked.

"Nurse?"

Nurse hurried over. "Yes Ma'am?" Already holding out her arms to take the child.

"Have you notice anything about Maurelle recently?"

Nurse shook her head. "No, Ma'am. She is her usual bonny self. A happy wee girlín to be sure."

"Oh, it's nothing," Alvina muttered, "just a trick of the light."

Maurelle squirmed in her arms as if she was not happy at being stopped in her game.

"Yes, perhaps baby is ready for bed now," she said handing Maurelle to Nurse.

Nurse took the wriggling bundle and quickly left the room.

~

Twyford signaled with a short downward flick of two fingers. They knew what it meant: Stop and ne'er a sound. He breathed in deeply, stared with intensity through the tall swaying fir trees as the high wind caught the upper branches. They creaked and groaned as if moaning out warnings to the men. *Don't Don't Don't*

He gestured for the party to spread out. Like a bloodhound, Twyford knew how to pick up a scent. Follow it to its core. All the time scanning, searching, smelling. His inner senses sure to go a-prickling when they were near. But had his senses failed him? He neither saw nor heard nor felt their presence. Ready now to call a halt he took one last sweep of the area, about to turn away.

A flicker. A trail of something...color?

A whiff… faint yet he knew exactly what it was.

Twyford immediately indicated with his hands.

Forward Now. Fast. Keep Going.

Never give them time to muster their power. Speed and ferocity were the hunter's weapon. That and Trowbridge's ability to sniff them out.

The hunters raised their weapons, unleashed their dogs and yelled in triumph.

As they sprinted through the forest, Twyford roared at them.

"Give them no time. Time will aid their faculties! Their power— the savage wind—the vicious fire if they can get it—rock surely. Beware! And run! Run!"

The wind surged, becoming a howling gale. Fir trees bent fiercely, first one way, then another. One older man, legs bowed, was not so quick. Catapulted by the unseemly force, a tentacle-like branch, with barbarous power, whipped his arm, severing it.

Twyford had seen this before. He yelled at the men again. "Onward. Don't stop."

Pointing to the small glade where a thin trail of smoke showed a recently extinguished fire. Fire.

"Quick now!" Twyford bellowed.

They spread out, weapons at the ready. Pitchforks, scythes, giant fish hooks, anything a man could carry and wield. Twyford gripped the worn stock of his whip, leather lash at the ready. The other hand held tight to the handle of his Lefaucheux. A harl or two it'd cost many moons ago. But the six shot barrel with its pinfire cartridges could shoot with speed and some accuracy. He would need it.

To his left, a puff of light and a gorse bush sizzled and coughed, then burst into life, blazing with intensity. The men near it screamed in agony as the fire seared their clothing, melting it to their skin.

"This way! This way!" roared Twyford.

Now, he was all sinew and senses, brute force and aggression. Animalistic. Gone his airs and graces. How easy it was to return to this state, this baseness. As if it always lurked in the dark corners of his soul. But the men instinctively followed him. They knew this was no place for civilized life.

Screaming their battle cry in defiance of their own fear, they broke through into a glade and before them the monsters. Only a few. Perhaps ten. But they were frenzied. They moved as if one, hissing and spitting. Their eyes flamed blood red in fury. Their matted, dirty hair writhed in the twisting air, air that was thick with stinging pine needles. Rocks flicked by the men's ears, cutting some, flattening others.

The females screamed in a rage of such ferocity it echoed through the clearing. Their frenzy whipped up the air and its contents to a state of violence. The hunters put their heads down, as if into a blizzard, and tried to shield themselves as pine needles punctured skin. Grit and sticks blinded them.

The male ones hurled large boulders in their direction, grunting in effort. The impacts cratered the ground.

Twyford never stopped pushing forward trusting the men to follow him. Some would be lost, but this was a battle that must be won. He flung his whip over his head and cracked it like a lightning rod on the biggest one. The creature howled. A bloody streak slashed across his face. The other creatures bellowed as if calling all the elements to protect them. Too late. Twyford leveled his gun.

~

Twyford let himself into the sleeping house. A small light burned in the hall to guide him. He was weary now, bone weary.

Every muscle ached. He grew soft and older in the last years. He clutched the railings as he pulled himself upstairs.

Midway up, he paused.

Something yet nothing. As if the tiniest pebble had been dropped in the center of a large lake, created a ripple that undulated out, decreasing in power until it vanished. He sniffed slowly and deeply. A frown creased his grimy brow.

For some moments he stood very still. But then he shook his head and continued. Exhausted by the hunt, his senses were frayed. Hyper and raw, feeling things that were not there. He stopped on the landing to listen intently at the nursery and in between Nurse's snoring he could hear a smaller gentler breath.

All was well. His family slept. They were safe. His duty done. He protected them as he protected their world. So they could sleep a sleep of innocence. They need not be burdened by…

His hand rubbed at his tight neck. Tight from using muscles grown weak in his years of playing normal. He used them this night as he lashed out with his whip. Bringing their leader to a halt. Blood a river on that face. His eyes blood red also, from an inner light. Such hatred. And something else.

Twyford shook himself. Dog tired, he was imagining things. He endeavored to compose himself. Right himself. In the anteroom, he stripped off his stained clothing and stood there naked. He grimaced for his stench intermingled with theirs. After splashing water on his face and along the back of his neck, he ran a rag to the stink of his pits, his groin. He scrubbed hard.

⁓

Alvina wakened. Twyford was home. She sat up in the bed and quietly called to him.

A few moments later he opened the door, cotton nightshirt barely coming to his knees. His damp hair curled around his shoulders. Neck muscles protruded.

Sometimes Twyford looked so big. It really was a wonder how she of all the girls, she who was destined for some scented gentleman, managed to snag such a rugged man. But he wormed inside her heart until he consumed her whole being and no one else existed for her.

Alvina remembered the first time she saw Twyford. Another boring evening party with the usual faces. Then he appeared. The dark, brooding man loomed over every other in the room. He was decked out in ill-fitted garments as if borrowed from a much smaller man, but something in the hardness of his face, the solemnity of his gaze, commanded attention. Compared to him, the sweet chattering young men paled to insignificance, appearing weak and foppish in her eyes. Her heart had skipped a beat.

She tried not to pay him a blind bit of notice. Yet she couldn't help it. Her eyes drawn to him by some strange magnetism. She caught his eye. A frisson, almost a fear pulsed through her. But Alvina was not one to give in to silly girlish foibles. She stuck her head up, pursed her lips, and examined him. He returned her look with a hard stare. And, as if this was the most important game she'd ever played, she refused to look away. He broke the contact. How she laughed.

Despite Papa's ranting and raving, and her poor mother's pleas and tears, she was not to be denied. Thumbing her finger at the world, her father said. A saucy wayward minx, her mother cried.

Ultimately, her parents were defeated by her will. Her resolution. In the end, they decided to make the best of it. The elegant little notice issued and the world was told of their union.

Not many saw him in the bedroom, unearthed and laid bare. Alvina held her arms out to him.

Twyford smiled indulgently, gently caressing his wife's hair as she told him about her day. Maurelle was a delight, she told him, the little girl constantly chatted away with nonsense words, which Nurse seemed able to interpret. He held her until sleep claimed her once again.

~

Twyford eased Alvina down into the pillows. And quietly left the room.

Still that trail of a scent. Had he brought their stench home? Perhaps it was merely his nerves, raw from tuning in to his inner senses, which made him feel so on edge. But he learned over years of probing and searching, how hints and suggestions often proved correct. Dangerously so.

He glanced around but was assailed by the deeply scented bowls of floral arrangements placed in the hallway. Alvina loved her flowers and plants. Nurse assured her it helped filter the dirty air from town. This was especially important now there was a baby in the house. The aroma reminded him where he was. His home. His sanctuary. He shook himself. He was no longer on the hunt. Not here.

Sitting in the library, poking the embers of a fire, Twyford tapped out the ash from his clay pipe, its intricate carvings a memory of times before. He packed in fresh tobacco and, from a small sachet tied to a cord around his neck, he carefully took a naps worth of mountain mandrake. With a stick glowing from the fire, he lit the pipe. Slowly, he breathed in the dark smoke, curling it around his mouth and throat.

The mandrake snaked its sinuous way through his aching body. It soothed raw nerves that felt frayed and exposed. His muscles loosened. The pain in his shoulder and neck eased. His mind calmed. He reflected on how much happier Alvina was again. Like the young bride once more. Full of endearment and welcome for him. He took another deep pull from his pipe and let his breath out slowly.

It was worth the effort he'd made to get Maurelle. The dangerous and illegal game he played, giving up a sackful of harls to win a golden-haired baby. So lucky to get one so young. And so beautiful and sweet. All his wife could ever wish for. It made their life complete. The missing element finally found, ensuring his wife's contentment, and his peace.

Nurse found her for him and, what fortune! Nurse so attached to the little child that she wished to stay with her. It made the transition seamless. Their entry into the house an easy addition. The baby never fussed. His wife no longer brooded in her room or glared at him with resentment. Now she was bright and carefree.

Yes, it had been worth it.

But before the mandrake finally drew him into sleep, his mind flicked back to the hunt that night. The heart-thumping chase through the woods. The prickling of his senses so that he felt shot through with adrenalin as he and the men thundered past everything they flung at them.

Surely now the threat was gone forever. How would the monsters carry on after this last slaughter? Twyford Trowbridge had lived up to his reputation. He should be well satisfied.

So why did he feel so dissatisfied? So hollowed out? Why the niggling feeling deep within?

Twyford thought once again to the leader of the pack. Knowing he was defeated, he mustered all the wind and flung as much debris at them as he could. Light them up if they could, but they were well outnumbered and cornered. Weakened by long years of flight and isolation.

And yet...

Twyford could not say. If he had to put words to the look, the message in those eyes as they stared at him in its final moments, was hatred, defiance, and pride, even in his ultimate defeat. And, yes, he had to admit and the mandrake, possibly giving him the insight he didn't have earlier, what he finally saw in the monster's eyes, as he leveled his gun at him was triumph.

~

Nurse sat in the corner, her gaze switching between the night sky and her small charge. She knew what transpired that night. It winged its way through the dark sky. Terrible tales of destruction, pain, sadness.

Sacrifice.

She was unhinged, yet wholly resolved. Grimly so. To be the last Protector, charged with continuing the bloodline that was hated yet must be preserved. As incontrovertible as nature, the undeniable dark to their light. A thousand year bond the people sought to withdraw from. How ignorant and ultimately weakened by it they would be. They could only suffer in the end.

One day Nurse knew they would be needed again.

~

"It is our pleasure to tell you, dear People,

a **Victory** *has been gained over an*

Insidious, Devious

gathering of our hated

ENEMY.

~

Our illustrious **Majesties**

have declared a public holiday called

TROWBRIDGE DAY

in honor of our

HERO *of the Day.*

§

Extract from the 'Daily Universal Advertiser,' by kind permission.

Maurelle stirred from her slumber, kicked off her covers, and started to gurgle to herself. Nurse smiled. She peered into the cot, placing a fresh bunch of lavender beside the child.

"Awake my little one?" Nurse's eyes gleamed, a hint of violet glinting around the iris. Maurelle returned her gaze. The child's normally gray eyes were briefly pierced by a plummy crimson. Maurelle chirped happily and held out her arms.

Nurse touched the baby. An arc of vermillion light sparked between their hands. Maurelle squealed in delight. Nurse picked up and hugged her charge. She whispered soft words into the small ear.

Maurelle sighed as if she understood. The baby gazed at the candle flame as it flickered in its holder. Her little finger pointed at it and drew back. The flame oscillated from side to side as if caught by a breeze. Maurelle pointed up, and it followed her lead, the luminescence leaving the wax stick and hovering in the air.

Nurse smiled but gently curled her hand around the smaller fist, and the flame returned to the candle.

Nurse looked at Maurelle and she spoke softly. "Not yet, sweet child. Not yet. We hide ourselves where they will never think to look…"

Nurse and Maurelle turned to gaze out at the darkness of the night.

"We must be silent, precious Maurelle. For now."

Their eyes glimmered, fleetingly, a blood-red radiance.

STONES

BY STAR GREY

1ST PLACE INITIATE AWARD WINNER

The air in the warehouse filled Grey's nose with the stale stench of copper and cedar. He hid behind munitions boxes with his sister, Raven, watching. Two guards in BeneCorp camouflage uniforms stood on either side of Ashe, holding him still. Lord Alvin sat in a chair, a marksman at his side. Ashe's wrists were bleeding, and his face was swollen. Grey calculated his chances of taking them all out.

"You broke your oath to this organization," Lord Alvin said. "It fills me with sadness. I had high hopes for you."

Grey tried to move, his heart pounding. He had to save Ashe. Raven's hand closed on his arm, and she shook her head. They would all die if he tried.

"Fire when ready."

The gunshot rang out, and Ashe's body fell to the ground. Red and hate filled Grey's vision. He tried to pull away from Raven, but her grip was firm. They had to leave. Somewhere in his mind he knew it was true, but he couldn't bring himself to do it. If Lord Alvin found out they knew about this, Raven would be next. They needed help. *I'll find the Refugees*, he promised Ashe. *Then I will kill Lord Alvin myself.*

~

Grey watched his sister. Raven sat on her cabin bed arms crossed tightly over her chest, tears in her blue eyes as the others helped her. She gave Grey a terrified look as the others surrounded her to attempt removing her Control. This was going to hurt.

Grey looked down. It was only her trust in him that kept her sitting, allowing Lucy to work slowly, her fingers pressed into Raven's scalp. The BeneCorp Control was vicious, like a net weaving over the mind with hooks to keep it in place. It was like trying to untie an impossible knot. Sweat beaded Lucy's brow. Grey dug his fingernails into his palms as she whimpered. He hadn't really believed they could free Raven and her powers. *Sheer, dumb luck,* he thought.

Raven's Control was different than what Lucy had removed from other refugees. Raven wasn't an automaton. They'd simply put a lid on her powers so that she couldn't harm anyone outside of the call of duty. Grey watched them put Control on her after they returned from a bounty hunt where she accidentally started half a town on fire. BeneCorp was afraid of the attention she would attract to their work.

Grey struggled to watch Lucy. It was intricate work, removing the web of Control strand by strand from the brain without harming the victim. Every time she screamed or started to sob in pain, he felt the pain with her. Tears welled in his eyes as he watched.

"If this kills her—"

"Calm down, Grey," Gordon said. He stood near the cabin door, hand on his holstered pistol. The weapon wasn't to protect the cabin from invasion. It was intended for use on Raven should she snap and turn on them. Sometimes, Lucy had explained, a surge of power lashed out once the Control was gone if the victim was scared enough. Grey knew Gordon would put Raven down like a rabid dog if she lashed out at them with her power. "We've all done it. Ain't no one died yet."

That was hardly reassuring. Grey had given up everything to save his sister. If she died here, he would have lost everything but the clothes on his back and his pistols. Pistols Gordon refused to allow in the cabin tonight. Grey hardly found that fair.

The process lasted just over an hour. Raven sobbed and screamed throughout, her back arching as if in the throes of death. Grey hated seeing her like this and took satisfaction from the fact that Lucy appeared to be suffering as well. Exhaustion ringed her eyes. Sweat beaded her brows. She seemed ready to collapse.

Finding Control on a mind was Lucy's gift. She learned how to use it to remove Control. A few months back, Grey would have turned her in to them without thinking twice.

"It's done," Lucy said, at last, letting go of Raven's head and laying her on the bed. Raven had passed out from the pain five minutes ago. Pain had never bothered Raven before. She was tougher than most men Grey knew.

Lucy wobbled on unsteady feet as she moved toward the door. Her friend took her arm to help her along.

"She will likely sleep for a full day as she recovers," Lucy said. The weakness was also in her voice. "But the Control is gone. It was incredibly complicated." She gave Grey a weak smile. "I believe she tried to fight them off."

Grey nodded. "Thank you for helping her."

As Lucy left the room with her friend, Grey made his way to the bed to tuck Raven in properly.

Gordon shuffled his boots. "I'll just stand watch outside the door."

Watch, Grey thought. *Not protect. Watch.*

~

Grey crouchs behind a boulder on the rocky tundra, inspecting the enormous pyramid rising from the cracks in the ground. Three of the structure's four sides resemble the plain on which it stood, without entrance. It's the perfect cover for BeneCorp—out in the middle of nowhere, hidden by the natural camouflage of the landscape. Undetectable. Impenetrable.

Until today.

Only one entrance leads into the secret headquarters—straight through the front gates. Unless, of course, you'd spent your childhood exploring the headquarters, like Grey. He has no intention of walking right in. Stealth is his ally. Stealth and his two pistols.

Grey's target clears in his mind's eye. Lord Alvin Winchester-Underhill, BeneCorp CEO.

"So where is it?" A deep, familiar voice drifts over his shoulder. Sergeant Gordon Rowland-Gravely is the only person in the world he trusts now. It gives him a boost of confidence to have Gordon at his back through this.

Grey squints into the setting sun, seeking the secret entrance he and his brother Ashe had once discovered. They kept it between them, but he is sure the heads of BeneCorp knows it is there too. "There." He points at what looks like a sharp, angular boulder against the western flat wall of the pyramid.

Gordon leans close as he squints at the boulder, a familiar deep-set frown on his face. "Well, what we waiting for then?"

Gordon shifts the pistol holstered on his hip and moves at a stealthy crouch toward the entrance. Grey grins as he follows. Together, they move quickly and quietly toward the boulder.

~

The main dining hall of the *N.S.S. Storm* was darkly lit, with paneled walls that reflected the dim light. A few people sat together at tables, eating, drinking, and talking. When he boarded the airship with Raven to help her escape BeneCorp, he had expected a group of roughly dressed, run-down vagrants. Instead, ladies wore proper dresses with high necklines and layers of lace. The men wore a mix of military uniforms and well-cut coats with long lace cuffs that spilled from the sleeves. According to his new friend, Sergeant Gordon Rowland-Gravely, the airship was turned in for salvage. Refugees who fled from BeneCorp—mostly consisting of ex-military men who were once under Control, a form of brainwashing, by the organization—rescued the airship from its fate. They fixed it and began sailing the skies around the world to find others who, like themselves, were hunted by BeneCorp.

Grey sat across a small, round table from Gordon. There were some fascinating people on this ship, but none so much as his current companion.

BeneCorp was one of the oldest organizations in the world. They were renowned for the medicinal goods they produced to help those in need. Grey was raised around the headquarters for the organization, though, so he knew what really happened.

"In the underground labs, they made magic-users compliant with Control," Grey explained as Gordon swirled his brandy glass. "A few who had valuable fighting skills were turned into soldiers for BeneCorp. The goal was to extract magical powers and find ways to turn those powers into controllable weapons."

"I'm aware of what they did," Gordon said flatly.

"But you don't understand why I did it," Grey said. "After what happened to our parents—after they were killed by someone out of control of their powers—we were eager to serve as bounty hunters. People who couldn't control their magic made us sick. It was sort of like… a personal duty to see that dangerous magic-users were under Control… until Ashe." Grey looked down into the golden liquid, the corners of his mouth turning downward.

"Ain't many on board this ship who'd take kindly to you if they knew what you just told me." Gordon swished his whiskey. "Dangerous stuff. I'd keep a lid on it if I was you."

Grey smirked. "Aw, lighten up, Gordy. I have just as much reason as anyone else here to hate BeneCorp. They killed my brother. They tried to Control my sister."

"It's Gordon," he said, then took a swig of his drink. A dangerous glint shown in his eyes. "Alls the same, keep it to yourself much as you can. There's people on this ship who'd kill you as soon as look at you if they knew."

Grey rolled his eyes. No one was as lucky as him. It was a gift. Instead of pressing the issue, he leaned across the table and flashed his best smile. "Except you, Gordy."

"Gordon. And I'm not proud of the work I did for that organization either. Controlling me like a puppet. Making me kill. But there's the difference between you and me. I never volunteered for the job like you did."

Grey's charming smile didn't waver. He merely shrugged it off. "No one's perfect. At least I came to my senses, Gordy."

Gordy scowled at him and clenched his jaw. "I was under their Control, a puppet assassin. Then they send me out after a mark…" Gordy down a drink and looked at his nearly-empty glass with longing for more. "My sister. See, she was a maid at this lord's manor. When her magic kicked in, she learned things about him what caused a right bit o' trouble. We tried to run, but the only way ta save 'er was to let them catch me." He grazed his teeth over his lower lip. "Wasn't 'til I tried catching 'er as a mark I saw 'er ag'in. Lavinia was with these here refugees. It was 'er what broke me from Control." He rubbed a hand through his red hair. "Hurt like hell."

⁓

The tunnel is narrow and dark, lit only by the filtering of light from the room ahead. The darkness doesn't bother Grey. He knows this tunnel. He, Ashe, and Raven used it several times to sneak in and out for a little adventure when they were young. It's familiar to him, like coming home again. The damp smell of stone comforts him.

At the mouth of the tunnel, a round grate bars the entrance. "Gordy, hand me the magnet." While he waits, Grey peers through the grate to make sure the room is empty. This room is usually unoccupied, but it's best to be safe.

The magnet touches the sleeve of his leather coat, and Grey reaches back. It's slow work unscrewing the bolts with the magnet from inside, and he has to stop periodically to check that they are still alone. Sweat trickles down his forehead. The breeze moving through the tunnel from outside isn't enough to cool him off. The only sound is that of his heart beating in his ears, and the occasional soft sound of Gordon breathing behind him.

Gordon is exceptional at being silent, a former military man by little more than title.

The grate comes loose with the last bolt, and Grey carefully lowers it to the ground in front of the tunnel so they can slip inside. His boots thud softly on the concrete floor as he crouches through. It's disturbingly quiet in this room. The hairs on his arms rise. Grey moves aside and waves Gordon inside.

While Grey replaces the grate, Gordon crosses the room to the door, taking cover behind the pallets of goods and metal boxes. He presses his ear to the hallway door and listens for noise. Grey breathes in the familiar smell of copper and cedar that fills the entire BeneCorp HQ. But it reminds him of Ashe's final moments now.

"Set these," Gordon says, extending three explosive charges in his hands. They won't go off without the trigger, tucked safely in his pocket.

Grey takes them and makes quick work of it around the room. Yes, it's indeed like coming home again, except he doesn't have Ashe leading him along, or Raven at his shoulder. *Raven. I will get you outta here before they harm you.* He won't lose his little sister, too. BeneCorp will pay for messing with the Stones. Grey will blow this entire place to the ground.

～

"Everyone just hear him out!" Gordon's voice thundered over the arguments that arose in the main dining room of the airship. He currently held Grey's guns, more for the reassurance of the crowd than anything else

Everyone onboard the airship gathered to hear Grey's plan to get Raven back and take down BeneCorp once and for all. As Gordon had warned, very few people actually trusted him once they found out he once worked for the organization as a bounty hunter.

"It's because of him and his family that the company exists," said Elden, an older man with gray hair at his temples.

"He's the reason we're on this ship in the first place," said Maryanne, a handsome woman with broad shoulders and a permanent scowl.

Grey's hands balled into fists, and his jaw twitched as they all argued against him. The nerve they had! Everyone in this room had suffered at the hands of BeneCorp, himself included. Grey came clean, told them that he had worked for the organization, that he had been loyal to them until they killed his twin brother, Ashe—until they tried to take Raven from him. He explained the entire story, and instead of embracing him, they sounded like a lynch mob, ready to string him up by his neck.

"They took my sister!" Grey's anger bubbled to the surface. "They put Control on her to keep her from using her abilities. They threatened her, forcing us to run. We came to you for help. For a chance to start over and right our wrongs. They snuck on board *this ship* and took her right from under all of our noses!" He stabbed a finger at Elden. "How would you feel if they did that to your wife?"

Kara's eyes widened, and she clung to Elden's arm. The idea of being taken back by BeneCorp was terrifying to all of them. They would lose control of themselves, attack their own family and friends, become lab rats. They would be automatons—unable to think for themselves, live for themselves. Every single person here was touched by this experience. No one was an exception.

"How long do you think you can cruise the clouds before they find you and take this ship down?" Grey felt his ears burn and his chest tighten. "I've lost just as much as any one of you. Maybe more than some. And I'm telling you, I can get us in, but I need your help."

"How do we know you aren't leading us into a trap?" asked Burke, a young former soldier who took a liking to Gordon's sister.

Grey scowled. "What do I have to gain?"

"You used to work for them, bounty hunter," said Maryanne. "Maybe you still do!"

"His plan is a solid one," Gordon interrupted. "We got enough ex-military here who know I'm right. And so is he." He stabbed a finger at Grey.

"You trust him, Gordon?" Lavinia asked. If anyone could be swayed, it was her. She could just read Grey's mind if she wanted. That would tell them the truth.

Gordon looked them over for a moment.

Grey held his breath. Why was he hesitating?

"I do," he finally replied. "With my life and yours."

"My life isn't yours to gamble," said Lucy, glaring at the two of them. "If you trust him, feel free to go, but we won't. If you go, you go alone."

"Go ahead and hide in the clouds like cowards then," Grey snapped. He snatched his pistols back from Gordon and headed toward the door, stuffing them in the hip holsters. "And if we fail because you didn't help us, BeneCorp will slip onboard and take each of you, one by one."

A swordswoman—Jucinda, he thought her name was—stood near the door, watching Grey with a critical eye. "Is that a threat?" she hissed as he passed.

He didn't bother responding.

Screw them. As long as he had Gordon, he could still manage this. He walked down the corridor toward one of the shuttles.

Gordon caught up at the steel door leading into the shuttle. His strong hand clamped around Grey's arm. "I'm comin'."

"You don't have to do this, Gordy," Grey said as he opened the door of the shuttle.

"I do, and you know it."

The look that passed between them was mutual, and Grey did know. If anything happened to him, Gordon would never forgive himself. It would haunt him to his grave.

～

Gordon stands beside Grey, their backs pressing against the wall in the brightly-light hallway.

"This don't seem too easy to you?" Gordon asks.

Two BeneCorp soldiers keep guard around the corner, talking and laughing, unaware.

Gordon's right. They're just walking right in. Are the guards waiting upstairs to capture the two of them? No one except the Refugees knows they are here. What about the surveillance?

"I told you I was lucky," Grey says. "Better for us, since we're only two." He gives Gordon a mischievous grin. "Let's have some fun."

"Me first," Gordon growls, then slips around the corner before Grey can speak.

No noise aside from two distinct thumps. Grey peeks around the corner and sees Gordon hauling the two guards toward a door by the collars of their camouflage uniforms. So far, they encountered only a handful of guards. Gordon dealt with them quickly, using BeneCorp's training against them. Grey killed a guard who tried to raise the alarm.

Once the two bodies are in the room, tied up and gagged, the two men move toward the hallway again. Grey peers out to make sure the coast is still clear, heart thumping against his ribs. He drops another charge in the room.

"This is it," Grey says. "Find her and bring her back to me."

"Let me go to the office, while you get her," Gordon says, again. "She'll respond better to you. Don't think she likes me."

"We'll have better luck this way, trust me."

Grey locks gazes with Gordon, whose eyes are hardened, but Grey sees the softness hidden underneath.

Holding the other man's gaze, Grey speaks again, persuasively and from his heart. "If there is resistance at the office I have a better chance at walking through the door than you do. They know me. I promise you my luck will work in our favor one way or the other."

Gordon scowls. He apparently isn't buying what Grey is trying to sell. He wants to be the one who puts a bullet between Lord Alvin's eyes. To destroy BeneCorp.

Grey puts his hand on Gordon's shoulder and squeezes. "Trust me."

Gordon's shoulder tenses, but he nods stiffly.

The two of them move out into the hallway to the fork where they would split. Gordon has the directions Grey gave him down to the labs where Raven will be. Grey will head toward Lord Alvin's office. Before parting ways, they give each other one last glance. Grey's chest tightens, and he silently wishes Gordon well. Maybe he has more than just Raven to lose now.

The ground shakes as a thunderous boom resounds throughout the pyramid. Grey stops in his tracks and looks around, hands on his pistols. "Gordy…"

His companion is at the other end of the hall. A grin blooms on his face, eyes cast at the ceiling. "They decided to trust you after all, Grey Stone. You *are* one lucky bastard."

Way to sound the alarm, guys, he thinks.

Grey hopes for one last glance at Gordon before they both run off. "Gordon!" He pulls his pistols with lightning-quick reflexes and opens fire on the guards running up behind Gordon. The shots ring out, hitting the guards. *No sense in stealth now.*

The hallway erupts in gunfire from all sides as the two of them are boxed in. The pyramid shakes again. Grey and Gordon find themselves pressed back to back. The Refugees are screwing up his plans.

"On three, go low and get out," Grey says over his shoulder as he fires off defensive rounds.

"But—"

"Stick to the plan, Gordy." Grey holsters one of the guns and pulls a flashbomb from inside his coat.

Brilliant light flares up, but Gordy and Grey protect their vision. Gordon follows up with a smoke bomb. The guards open fire on the two of them, and they both duck low to slip out in opposite directions through the smoke.

With the pyramid under attack, the halls fill with guards scurrying to get to their stations. Smells of mortar, gunpowder, and copper fill Grey's nostrils. He leaves a trail of charges in his wake and finds himself caught up in more than one fight. It means killing. The only difference between the men and women here against those on *N.S.S. Storm* is that they don't know they are being used—the Refugees know who they are fighting and what they are fighting for.

Hopefully, when this is all done, everyone will be free from BeneCorp, he thinks, stepping over a young female officer who attempted to draw him down and lost.

A boom resounds from inside the pyramid. Grey presses his back to the hallway wall, heart in his throat. BeneCorp is fighting back. All those people who counted on him are going to die. Grey closes his eyes and takes a few calming breaths. Nerves are bad for his good luck. He exhales and peeks around the corner into the adjoining hall.

Ten guards stand outside the office door at the end of the junction, all pointing pistols down the hall. He can't blast through all of them. The pyramid trembles and more dust breaks free from the ceiling. He shakes the debris from his hair.

Grey clicks on the safety for each pistol and flips them into the holsters. He lets out a breath, calming his nerves. *This is it.* He steps around the corner with his hands up. In seconds he is surrounded, disarmed, and bound at the wrists.

"Let me see him," Grey says. "I just want to know what he did with Raven."

They don't seem alarmed by his request. In fact, they are headed toward the office door even as he asks. *It shouldn't be this easy.*

The door opens, and he's pushed inside. Lord Alvin. At last. He will turn over Raven and pay for what he did to the Stones. Grey's heart hammers against his ribs, jars his teeth. *Not the nerves.* This is the worst time for his luck to run out. He tries to take a deep breath.

Despite the commotion outside the office, the inside is peaceful. Only the occasional boom and shake of the building—accompanied by more debris from the ceiling. The familiar scent of orange oil and mahogany fill the air. The only light comes from the desk lamp, casting a strange light on the light gray walls and making the dark wood floor almost seem to glow. Grey feels at home in this familiar setting.

The high-back leather chair behind the mahogany desk is turned away from him. Hands press on his shoulders, holding him in a painful vice grip. That natural easiness settles over him again.

The chair creaks and the leather seat squeaks as the occupant turns. Inner calm shatters.

"Excellent work, Grey," Ashe says, leaning his forearms on the desk. "Exactly according to plan." He's grinning. "You're brilliant."

The sight of his brother knocks the wind from Grey's lungs. Everything inside of Grey explodes into thousands of pieces. *Ashe is alive?* He doesn't know if he should cry for joy or be terrified.

"But how? I… I saw you die."

"Oh come on, Grey. The jig is up." Ashe looks pleased.

"I saw you die."

"You saw what you needed to see in order to remember what you needed to remember." The look in Ashe's eyes gives Grey chills.

Is this familiar?

Grey blinks, trying to pull back the memories. Bile rises to his throat. But he remembers. Ashe refused to kill one of the Marks. A girl. *Maggie.*

Just the memory if watching them shoot Ashe brings out all the pain and rage again. Grey's head spins. "I don't understand. I saw them kill you."

Ashe walks around the desk. "Cut him loose. He won't be killing anyone in this office."

The guards remove the bonds and step back.

Grey rubs his wrists.

Ashe puts his hands on either side of his brother's head then kisses his forehead. "Let me help you remember."

Grey cries out as pain lashes in his head. It's hard to hear. Hard to understand. Hard to focus.

"These Refugees have grown too many," Ashe says, holding Grey's head in his palms. "Our men would go out on missions and never return. Those that the Refugees couldn't turn were killed. So you came up with a plan."

Something snaps in Grey's mind. He would have crumpled to the floor if Ashe didn't catch his arms. A cry escapes. His mouth goes dry.

"I have to say," Ashe says, giving Grey's shoulders a light squeeze, "when you first proposed this wild plan, I had my doubts. But the Mind Control worked. It allowed you to infiltrate them without drawing any suspicion. Allowed you to uncover their underground, which it turns out was nowhere underground." Ashe smirks, clearly amused by that fact.

Grey struggles to get a grip on himself, the room still unbalanced. "What are you talking about?"

Ashe releases Grey and perches on the edge of the desk, his arms across his chest as he continues. "I can see you're still not thinking clearly. You see, we discovered they could detect the Control marks that we put on them and remove them, thus liberating those that you and I worked so hard to capture. Since my ability was different from what BeneCorp typically used, you figured it would be virtually undetectable."

Grey is suffocating. He can't draw breath as his memories war with each other, threatening to break him apart. Two different versions of himself fight for control: one that remembers his hate for the organization, the other that remembers growing up with Ashe and taking over operations. Some part of him wants both to be true. Grey lets out a sick groan and squeezes his eyes shut to try and get a grip. Tears roll down his cheeks. *It isn't true. It can't be!* Grey's eyes open again as his brother continues.

"All we had to do was put you under my personal Control so that you remembered only what I wanted you to remember, stage my execution so that you believed BeneCorp had betrayed you and put Control on Raven so you would have a reason to fight against us."

Ashe's laugh rips through Grey's inner war.

"With Control on Raven," Ashe continues, "you also could become a sympathizer to the Refugees. They would want to liberate Raven just like anyone else they found."

Raven! "What did you do to her?" Grey growls. "Where is she?"

"Oh, she's perfectly safe." Ashe waves it off.

Lines of torture crease Grey's usually smooth features. He

only feels betrayal. Everything else mixes in a vortex of emotional confusion, clouding his judgment.

"And Lord Alvin?" he breathes out, hardly able to get the name off his tongue.

"Died tragically two years ago," Ashe says.

Died! Grey would have gasped for breath if he could have.

"Fortunately for us, he left everything in our name. You and me. The Brothers Stone ready to take over the world one magic-user at a time." Ashe looks triumphant.

... Ashe sat in the dark office, smoking a cigar with his boots on the mahogany desk. Lord Alvin never allowed them in his office to lounge like this. Grey sat in the chair across from him, Raven on the arm beside Grey. "To the old codger's untimely demise," Grey said, lifting his brandy glass. He knew what Ashe had done. It didn't matter. Not after what Lord Alvin did to Raven. "May we succeed where he so terribly failed." The other two joined in the toast...

Boots thump against the wooden floor behind him, coming through the office door.

"He looks like shit," Raven says. She walks past Grey and stands beside Ashe.

Grey shook his head to clear his vision.

"You said he wouldn't get hurt by this."

"He's fighting it." Ashe waves off Raven's concern. "Work your influence. Maybe that'll help. You always had a way with him."

"Grey," Raven says, taking his hand and pressing it to her cheek.

It brings a small level of calm to Grey, but not enough.

"Don't fight it. It's me. I'm okay. Ashe is okay. Everything is fine. Just let go."

He lowers the hand from her face.

She leans closer and kisses him on the lips. A sweet, soft kiss. Familiar. So familiar. He starts to return the kiss, nearly losing himself in her lavender scent. "I'm not your sister, Grey. I'm your wife. And I had to watch you on that airship flirting and sowing your oats to your own delight. It took everything in me not to kill every one of them."

Then something in Grey snaps. It happens so fast. His hands slide up between her arms and knock them away, shoving her back into the desk, which then slides an inch across the floor. Folders, pencils, and rubber stamps clatter from it. Raven cries out. The sound rings in his ears. Grey lunges at Ashe to put his hands around his brother's neck and snap it. *This is a trick. All of it!*

But Ashe doesn't flinch. A strong hand wraps around his own throat. The wind knocks out of his lungs as his back slams into the wall. His feet dangle a few inches off the ground.

Gordon's dark eyes watch him, empty. *No! Not Gordy!* He tries to grab at Gordon's hand, but he's far too weak in comparison. "Please," he rasps. "Gordy, it's me." He claws at Gordon's arm. "It-it's Grey." *They wouldn't kill me… would they?*

"Disgusting," Raven spits at the two of them.

Ashe chuckles. "I applaud his dedication to the mission."

… Gordon was laughing at Grey, amused by his sense of humor. It was the first real smile Grey saw on Gordon's face. It filled him with a sense of joy. Something he was unfamiliar with…

Raven walks over to stand beside Gordon, looking at Grey with big blue eyes. "I would have preferred to kill him, but Ashe insisted that your new 'friend' was indispensable. Your relationship was a lie." Her pale lips curl up in the corners.

Grey is getting light-headed.

"But they're all mine now." She pulls out a knife and points the tip of it at the nape of Gordon's neck. Gordon doesn't flinch.

… It was dark outside. Grey and Raven were lying beside a boulder, staring at the empty sky. For the first time in his life, he felt like he was right where he should be. Raven raised her hand to the sky and lightning crackled across it, forming his name. Grey laughed and turned to look at her. Her face was as beautiful as the moon on a midnight ocean. Raven…

"Raven, stop!" Ashe knocks the knife away and looks at Gordon. "Let him down before he suffocates."

Gordon releases his grip on Grey's throat, and Grey collapses to the floor, gasping for breath. Before he gets control of himself again, Gordon pulls him to his feet with an arm twisted behind his back.

… "Why did you name your pistols?" Gordon was stretched out on the bed in Grey's cabin. He looked relaxed.

"Why wouldn't you?" Grey scratched his arm and poured himself another brandy. He turned to Gordon and held up the flagon.

Gordon shook his head.

"In my line of work, it's good to know the difference between Truth and Justice." He felt so relaxed around Gordon. As if he could just be himself. Ashe and Raven always made him work so hard to impress them…

Grey struggles to discern reality as the mortar around them continues to dust down with each boom. He has memories of his life before, of following Ashe around, trying to impress his brother.

He remembers Lord Alvin raising them from a young age, and how Raven was later adopted. He remembers how Ashe had been jealous of his relationship with Raven.

He remembers sitting in this very room, telling the two of them about his plan, hoping to win the admiration of his brother at last.

… The look on Ashe's face was priceless. As if he were staring at an endless mountain of gold, and it was all his. Grey puffed up a little. It wasn't often his brother admired anything he had to say. "You're really willing to do this, Grey?"

Grey just grinned. With his luck, they couldn't lose…

Ashe planted these other memories. Grey doesn't know what's real, except for one thing. "Gordy, listen to me," he rasps. "Remember me." He tries to look over his shoulder at Gordon.

… The cabin had a much less homey feel to it than some of the others Grey had spent time in on this voyage. That didn't mean he was any less at ease.

"I keep thinking about BeneCorp," Gordon said as he rummaged through his clothes to dress as if he would dress in anything other than his uniform. "If they ever found me again."

Grey poured two drinks and set the brandy bottle on the desk in the corner. "I would come." He handed one of the glasses to Gordon. "I'm not losing anyone else to them."

Gordon's eyes narrowed as he held the glass. "Why?"

"Why what?"

"Why would you come?"

Grey considered how best to answer this. "They can take people, but they can't take our memories. Not completely. Your freedom is proof of that. Your memories of your sister are what freed you, right?"

Gordon gave a slight nod.

Grey grinned and raised his glass. "Then remember me."

Gordon stared at him in a way that made Grey's stomach flip. For a moment he thought he would leave the toast hanging. "Remember me." Gordon raised his glass, and they drank.

Still, Grey couldn't shake the look that Gordon gave him. He hoped his luck held out and Gordon wouldn't punch him in the face. He liked his face. Grey leaned in and kissed Gordon…

"Oh hell, Gordy!" The muscles in Grey's arm strain painfully as Gordon pins behind his back. "Remember me, damn it!"

"Why are you fighting this, Grey?" Ashe crosses his arms and watches brother curiously. "Come on. Raven and I, we're your family. Not them. They mean nothing to us."

Grey shakes his head. "These memories aren't real." He's trying to convince himself as much as anyone else. The pain in his arm drives back waves of nausea and slows the spinning. He focuses on the pain, trying to regain some control.

The tears linger, and he feels fear—real fear—for the first time. "Gordy, remember me!" He can't listen to his brother. Listening to Ashe just sends his mind tumbling again. Everything Ashe told him makes him believe it's all planted. "No, Ashe. You've always despised me. This is a lie. All of it!" Grey says it out loud as much to convince himself as the others.

The grip loosens on his arm. Grey doesn't want to waste a second of opportunity. Only one way to know what's true.

"Grey, you're my brother," Ashe says. "I love you."

Grey pulls his arm free, grabs Gordon's pistol from the holster, and presses the barrel between Ashe's eyes. "Only one way to know for sure." If he kills Ashe, the fake memories will go away. He has to know what's real. Grey pulls the trigger.

The bullet goes straight through Ashe's skull, covering the desk with blood and shattered bone fragments. Raven lets out a shriek and reaches for a gun as Ashe's body falls to the ground. Grey hardly notices. His arm goes limp. Everything remains. The idea. The plot. The execution. The airship. Gordon.

Another shot rings in his ears and Raven falls to the floor. The room spins again. Grey's legs give out. Two strong arms catch him before he hits the floor. Gunshots ring in the hallway. Grey leans on Gordon, trying to shut everything else out. He loves his brother. He loves Raven. He loves Gordon. It can't all exist together. It's tearing him apart.

But this has to end.

Grey pushes off Gordon and stands upright, the expression on his face matching his surname: Stone. If Ashe is to be believed, then Grey has sole ownership of BeneCorp. "Let's shut this place down for good." The trigger to the explosives is still in his pocket.

Grey turns to the guards. "You heard my brother. This organization is mine. You fight for me. Go tell the rest."

The guards nod. So does Gordon. With Control still on their brains, they can't do anything but obey. *I will get that removed, Gordy. It will never happen again.* He's confident now, strong. Grey strides out into the hallway. Chunks of cracked tan stones litter the way, broken from the pyramid around them.

At the junction between the two hallways, steel bites deep into Grey's gut. Someone grabs his hair and shoves him to his knees.

"You betrayed us," snarls a woman's voice.

He looks up and recognizes the swordswoman, Jucinda, from the airship.

"I heard it all," she says. "You walked us right into a trap. This was all your idea. We lost men today."

Gordon is halfway down the hall already, but once he realizes what happened, he turns back.

Grey holds up a hand to stop him and tells her, "I did."

Blood pools beneath him. His hand shakes. He presses against the wound to little effect.

"We will leave here today, but you," she says. "You will stay. Welcome to your grave, Mr. Stone." She steps over Grey and disappears around the corner again.

Grey looks at Gordon as everything starts to fade. *This is no less than I deserve.* "Gordy. Help them escape. Help them all."

Gordy turns away and disappears around the corner.

Grey's weak. So weak. And cold. There's no way he's getting out alive. Grey pulls out the trigger and bows his head. Footsteps approach, crunching debris beneath boots. The stones from the ceiling start shaking free and fall around him. *An appropriate marker for my grave.* Grey closes his eyes.

He presses the trigger before it's too late. Sounds of explosions erupt as his body falls to the floor. The ceiling caves in.

The Stones buried in stone.

DIALLERS

BY PAUL PROFFET

That's it, folks. The whistle has blown, and the race is finished. The human race that is. If I'm able to get this printed, or you manage to fire up my laptop a hundred years from now, this is the eulogy for the people of planet earth. One final, definitive guide as to how we destructed as a species. I don't even know if I'll get to finish typing. The streets aren't safe whatever time of day it is, and the wretched survivors are impossible to fight off forever.

War didn't initiate Armageddon. The manufactured combat, instigated by billionaire racketeers was conspicuous in its absence. All the deadly bacteria were blameless too. We didn't make it long enough for the antibiotics to reach their threatened impotence. I'm also certain alien invaders and flesh-eating zombies never showed up either. Mores the pity.

It was a drug.

Although noble in the early stages, political correctness metastasized into a control mechanism for the masses. First, you couldn't say what you thought. Then it seemed you couldn't say anything at all without triggering some emotionally unstable asshole. Safe spaces and emotion shelters sprang up like psycho-nurturing vegetable patches. Within a few years, we had a whole generation of kids who couldn't cope with their feelings because they were encouraged to hide from them. I remember the news report vividly. A young student had failed his exams and was therefore certain his life had come to an abrupt end. The only warning he was dead was the expression of bafflement on his pallid face. He couldn't cope with the mythical belief he was ruined and suffered a catastrophic cardiac event. He died before he hit the campus tarmac.

Big pharma had been only too happy to help with a laundry list of options and the money-grabbing governments simply rubbed their hands with glee. The primary wave of drugs turned out to be rehashed versions of the stuff they had been pumping into kids to chase away the imaginary ADHD epidemic. It used to be called daydreaming when I was in short trousers.

The second wave was the real kicker. It worked on the emotional centers of the brain, numbing the rush of feelings to the point that even a fatal car wreck couldn't raise a reaction. Witnessing a fierce argument with a teacher or classmate wouldn't increase the user's pulse a single beat. Fear and despair became a thing of the past. The simple fact that love and empathy were also disappearing must have been buried in the small print.

The drug's full name was so long it was nigh-on unpronounceable, so the people just christened them 'Diallers.' Dialling down your pesky emotions became the go-to move for the drug-guzzling masses. The establishment seized the nickname believing it would make the horrific chemical cocktail far more acceptable. Mainstream media soon did their thing and whored themselves out to the drug companies, announcing the paradise Diallers promised. Doctors couldn't write prescriptions fast enough, and within a few short months, millions of fifteen to twenty-five-year-olds dialled worldwide. Even the military began hurling them down the throats of mentally damaged soldiers hoping to get a grip on the very real menace of PTSD.

I don't know if the side-effects were truly unexpected, or if the whole episode had been meticulously planned. Many of the internet based independent news feeds made dozens of scary claims. Before long, separating the signal from the chatter became impossible. The Crusaders screamed about what damage dialling caused, but the establishment didn't seem to care about the alleged evidence, and the Diallers no longer had the capacity to.

Social media finally dropped the hammer. Videos of terrible crimes committed by seemingly uncaring people went viral at the speed of five a day. No…not uncaring. That doesn't touch what I'm trying to convey. It doesn't have the gravity. They were oblivious. The thought that the acts they inflicted on other human beings were wrong didn't even enter their heads. Murderers and rapists were caught in the shameful act and seemed oblivious to their crimes.

A small percentage of the Diallers developed symptoms that terrified people the world over. At least the ones that weren't dialling themselves. The only needs that crossed their mind were linked with survival or lust. Impulse control was a distant memory, and if they chose to steal, kill, or rape another person, they just did it. Wherever and whenever they chose.

I remember the first case that made it to court. The young woman was incredulous at being dragged into the dock for strangling her mother. 'My dinner was late,' was the only thing she said. As if that mundane reason was enough to justify garrotting someone with an electrical cord in front of her three-year-old brother.

Things escalated rapidly until the cause of the malady was

discovered. We don't owe any thanks to a scientist or long-winded experiments. The clues were unearthed by a pissed-off marine veteran who converted a dialler's head into a canoe, utilizing a .44 magnum pistol he used for home defense. The twenty-year-old man had wandered into the veteran's house to take a flag displayed on the living room wall. Any notion he was stealing had been annihilated by the drugs coursing through his veins. The retired marine opened his side of the debate with a bullet and then rested. The opposition had nothing to add. Responding paramedics noticed a strange color in the center of the exposed brain and rushed him to a police lab. It took a police pathologist less than two hours to prepare a statement for the rest of us.

Over time, small deposits of the drug gradually calcified an area of the brain known as the pineal gland. The coating then went on to kill the gland and send the victim into a whole new realm of bastard. I read somewhere the ancients believed this gland to be the seat of the soul. The much vaunted third eye. Maybe it is… I don't know. But I'm certain of one thing. The victim became a degenerate savage acting however it saw fit. And its choices of activity usually involved pain and injury to anybody it encountered.

In the halcyon days of the previous century, any news of the discovery would have been suppressed completely. Not anymore. These are the days of the internet and information is king, baby. Word spread like a planet-wide hurricane. Keyboard warriors soon flexed their emaciated arms and warmed up their crooked fingers. They called the creatures 'Bricks', warning any avid listeners that if they realized someone had bricked they should avoid it at all costs.

I call them 'it' on purpose. Girls, guys, folks, whatever you choose didn't apply after that. They were vile specimens, unrecognizable to the rest of us. A few idiots preached that you could identify a brick by looking into its eyes. Windows to the soul and all that. A handful of eye-gouging incidents quickly shat on that plan.

Then things went right down the shitter. Remember the part where I said the military doctors doled out Diallers to manage PTSD. I'm sure some fat, old, cigar smoking asshole saw a great deal of potential in an army that didn't feel. I bet diseased minds even planned to take their show on the road. Oh yeah…try having an army of psychopaths who bricked in their thousands.

Read that last part again. Let it sink in for a while longer. Thousands of men and women, incapable of caring about anything and remove any impulse control they ever had. Next, select a few choice ingredients from a huge list of cutting-edge weapons and add to the mix. Stir well, then bring to the boil. You get the picture. Huge bases went off-grid overnight. Then the surrounding cities and towns.

One bonus-level dickhead came on TV pleading for calm. My incredulous inner monologue and screeching laughter almost drowned out the question he asked before the screen went dead. He screamed at the camera 'Why is it spreading so fast?' and he was right too. Even though millions watched their humanity flat-line, it still only made up a small percentage of the population.

Folks continued scratching their heads until the first non-dialler bricked. Her husband had taken the drug right up until being arrested for murder, but she managed to avoid it. Things came to a head a few days later when investigators realized bricking could also spread like a virus. The woman caught the soul-killing bullet from her husband like a sexually transmitted disease.

Society collapsed virtually overnight. Those weird recordings that were prepared to air during a nuclear war turned up on TV screens. My favorite was a public service warning showing a talk-show host begging the population to stay strong, although the flag waving type accompanied by a rousing military band popped up in most places that still had power. Within a few days, even those recordings changed to static and finally died. I used to wonder what the world would sound like with no unreality shows and screaming sports events. The screaming just got louder.

Dozens of super-rich industrialists disappeared as fast as their mega-bunkers could swallow them. They could be still down there now for all I know, swigging champagne and abusing servants. Things up here might not have affected them anyways considering most of them didn't have souls to begin with.

Those of us with the spirit to push on tried to organize ourselves so we could carve out some sort of existence, but it was way too late. Those living in urban areas made barricades and inner-city dwellers walled off their buildings in an attempt to hold Bricks back. But how do you plan for one of the defenders bricking in their sleep?

Anyone reading this could describe us as survivors of a global holocaust, but there's something you need to take into account before you slip on the rose tinted glasses. People can be considered survivors for all types of reasons, but most of those reasons are bad. Even those untouched by the drugs and their side-effects were likely to kill you for a can of beans or spoonful of gasoline. City streets descended into anarchy, and entire towns were purged of life and burned to ashes. The inherent lack of empathy bricking delivered meant those under the effects were just as likely to turn on others as they were surviving humans. Some people witnessed barbaric fighting with hundreds of combatants slaughtering each other until one or sometimes two exhausted killers remained.

With all the broken bodies strewn about the streets, the heat and summer winds stoked up a pestilence so virulent it killed thousands of Bricks and humans alike. We couldn't hope to hold the Bricks out forever, but when the plague came so did the end

I haven't heard an explosion for a few days, and the tower block down the street burned out. I risked a look between the wooden boards blocking the windows and saw a couple of Bricks marauding along the sidewalk searching for entertainment. Our building is battered and bruised, so they decided it wasn't worth the effort and moved on.

The lady on the top floor will draw them in at some point. The fever has taken her. Her moaning echoes down the stairwell sometimes. That's how you know they're in the final stages. Soon she'll be howling for respite, and the strangled shouting will draw the Bricks in. If there is any mercy left in this shitty little world, she will be dead before they start beating down her door. The Bricks I saw earlier were naked and splattered with gore. God only knows what they'll do when they find her.

It makes me chuckle sometimes to think how things have turned out. It wasn't laser-guided bombs or some new age Nano-virus. None of the warnings about self-aware AI wiping us out with chrome-plated robots happened either. Modern society was killed by a brick.

My mind is starting to wander. It may be due to the trauma of life right now, or the lack of food and clean water. I swear I heard Maurice bark the other day. He hasn't skittered around this apartment for over two years. I miss his lazy ass. Part of me wishes he was here to comfort me in the closing stages, but the rest of me is glad he isn't.

Feelings. It seems like such an inoffensive word now I type it. Eight letters that take up such a small amount of space on the page. But the power behind them is incredible. The fabric of humanity was stitched together by them, and when they started to die out, the blanket frayed and fell apart. I know people didn't necessarily restrain from inflicting pain on others out of love, but the fear of retribution was a feeling too. Now those emotions are gone. Burned up like the building down the street.

Well not inside me they aren't at least, not yet. When we stopped caring, we ceased to be human. All the love and hate, all the joy and grief. Learning to process all the emotions, both good and bad, was a critical stage in life. It's what pushed us onward and when the feelings died… we did too. We tried to control and kill off the very thing making us human. I see that now as I'm watching my last sunset creep past the cracks in my barricade. I know it's my last as I'm going to end things as soon as I type my final words.

But I'm not going before I say my piece to those of you reading this.

Thank you for pushing on and getting clear of this. Most of us left this broken planet because we tried to surgically remove something we should have celebrated. If you are reading these words, then you made it to the other side, and I love you for it. Yes, I said it… I love you. I still feel those things, and I hope you do too. Never stop loving people and your favorite places. Never stop getting frustrated at loved ones and also, lose your temper sometimes. It's good for the soul.

Please forgive us. Some of us had the guts to resist, but we didn't know the war was on until it was too late.

Ludo Beer
Taxi Driver

The Rake & the Headdress

By Kevin Martin

Layers of rugs covered the stone floor of the dark antechamber, dulling any noise. Tapestries aided the effect, but habit drove Alessia to proceed with caution to the waiting chair. The unseen walls made the room seem vast, and with each step she felt carefully for the floor as if she were on a tightrope. The room itself seemed to hold its breath before she reached the chair and sat down. It creaked, as always.

Light and warmth flowed into the room through the iron bars of the partition that enclosed the priory's visiting parlor; beyond, two candle stands stretched up from the bare stone floor and a cushioned armchair awaited, unoccupied. The underfloor heating, which worked in that part of the room, gave off a dry warmth. Reverend Mother liked her heat.

Alessia counted and recounted one hundred and seventy-eight flagstones in the stone floor as she waited. A sudden loud rattle of the latch broke the silence, then the door opened with a whisper, and the venerable prioress entered, preceded by a curious melange of perfume, beeswax, and a strangely masculine smell on which Alessia never dared to dwell. Her movements were difficult, an aged shuffle on fur-lined slippers. Reverend Mother sighed as she relaxed into the armchair, which grated slightly against the floor.

"Blessings to you, my dear Alessia." Her voice was a loud whisper, with a hint of a lisp.

"Blessings to you, Reverend Mother," Alessia murmured in response, trying to approach a whisper.

A grim smile split across the old woman's face. She leaned forward and whispered, with a hint of urgency in her voice. "My old friend, the count of Pariperte—we play cards every Wednesday. Oh, he deals so well, he has such lovely hands! Anyway, he intercepted, by accident, his youngest daughter on a furtive excursion to a scheming rascal. A rake. He charmed her with a series of flowery letters. If she reached the rendezvous, robbery of her jewels and despoiling of her purity awaited." Reverend Mother stopped. Her voice collapsed.

Alessia's hands went out to her, but stopped at the bars of the partition, clenching the cold iron. Memories rose, but she pushed them down. "Reverend Mother, I am listening. Who is this rake?"

"We do not know who he is. But we do know where he will be." Reverend Mother's voice hardened. "The count has confided in me, and we will not let him down. I have decided to continue with the rendezvous tonight. Alessia, my dear, you shall take the place of his daughter. Bianca waits in the hallway to give you a shoulder bag with jewelry and a distinctive headdress belonging to the count's daughter. You shall do the rest. Bianca and Livia shall go with you in the carriage and assist you afterward."

Reverend Mother tilted her face back so her broad forehead appeared in the dim light like a full moon revealed from behind clouds.

"I accept, Reverend Mother, but...." Alessia turned away from the steady gaze of the prioress.

Livia was a newcomer to the house, and the prioress was pushing her forward as an apprentice. Alessia winced, not looking forward to the additional burden of schooling a clumsy beginner on a mission dependant on subterfuge.

"Alessia, it is a favor, I know. Please take Livia with you. She has to learn some time." Reverend Mother's voice returned to a whisper, and she drew back into the shadows.

Alessia pushed herself slowly out of the chair and bowed her head. "Yes Reverend Mother, I agree."

⌒

In the dimly lit yard behind The Chandler's Tavern, Maltoni could not suppress a chuckle at his success. Claudia, the daughter of the Count of Pariperte, lay on the ground after the lightest of blows. Not a soul took notice. Nothing stirred in the breeze from the docks. No rats scuttled towards the kitchens. No reappearance of the stoat who bounded away earlier. Maltoni heard of snakes coming ashore once. Nothing surprised him when it came to foreign ships.

After one last look around, he knelt over her, his padded mace poised to strike in his right hand. He was breathing hard not from the exertion, but from the excitement of the chase. The unexpected reward of a fabulous necklace helped.

He'd played this one for months, and she was the fifth noblewomen to fall prey to the letters of that drunken sot of a would-be poet, Arnaud. She might be the last one for a while since Arnaud had failed of late to beguile any more young ladies into a correspondence, but she was a rare prize! He wished for more light to better see her face. Certainly, she was fairer than he'd expected when he'd espied her from afar. Soft, richly coiffed hair broke free from its elaborate headdress like a cushion under her head. It spread unevenly, and his fingers lingered as he stroked the long tresses and arranged them neatly over her shoulder. Her dress was as daringly cut as he'd hoped. She had taken all the hints he'd urged Arnaud to employ. The reveal of her left breast drew his hand under the fabric to feel its fullness. His palm tingled from the warmth of her skin.

For a moment he thought they sighed together. He realized too late that it was not the precursor to a greater intimacy. Her right hand shot up, and a curved blade plunged into his stomach. Her face came alive, the expression cold. He wondered for a heartbeat how a noblewoman could be in possession of such a cunningly designed weapon.

Then hot pain exploded inside him.

~

Alessia let go of the knife when the man jerked back. The pain on his face was almost enjoyable. He thoroughly deserved this, but killing at close quarters was a distasteful thing. She needed neither pleasure nor disgust at this moment.

When he recoiled again, as if trying to back away from the pain, Alessia pushed him off her legs and rolled into a crouch, taking stock. Two men rushed in from under the arch of the laneway. His accomplices. Her short sword glistened as she drew it from the hidden scabbard on her back without a whisper. Her free hand seized the mace from Maltoni in time to face them. They were armed, but they slowed to a stop upon sight of her, also armed and ready. Not overconfident then. They separated, one to the left, one to the right, as they gave themselves room to strike.

The one on the right raised a spiked club. Alessia faked to attack high, then dropped again to lunge toward his stomach, drawing a parry. As he tried to regain his footing, she sprang back to face the other, who was armed with a knife and clearly waited for an opening to strike. They faced each other a moment, and in that pause, the possibility of death seemed to take shape in the air above and around them.

Alessia's mouth was dry. Should the knifeman step back, he would throw. It was vital to keep him interested in making a strike, so Alessia again moved against the spiked club. Her feet were light, confident as she moved. Confidence not shared by her opponents. The man with the club jumped to one side to avoid the swift blade dancing first towards his left, then his right.

The knifeman shuffled sideways, attempting to get around and behind her. She fell into a crouch, sword punching upwards against the spiked club and, without looking in his direction, swung the mace sideways toward the knifeman's knees. He jumped back and overbalanced. Alessia lunged toward him, thrusting the mace up at his face, but she was at the extent of her reach, and the mace only threw him off balance.

The spiked club was swinging down at her head. With both her sword and mace, she deflected the heavy blow to the left. His momentum brought him toward her, and as she jumped to her right, she lost her footing. Alessia tucked and tumbled backward, using her left hand to bring her back to her feet. It forced her to drop the mace. All three of them looked at the mace.

Alessia adopted a look of resignation and let her left shoulder droop, allowing the strap of her dress to slide down her arm. Both men stared at her as she freed her arm from the strap and sought the long-necked jar of powders from the purse on her belt. This gave prominence to her state of undress, but she gambled that this simple artifice would befuddle her attackers. She damned the heavy embroidery as her fingers struggled to find the drawstrings on the unfamiliar purse.

As soon as she had oriented the jar, Alessia flung her hand toward the face of the knifeman, then threw the remains of the powder and the jar at the clubman. Its sharp pungency caused him to drop his guard, and the tip of Alessia's sword slid into his gullet with the precision of a weaver detailing a tapestry.

The knifeman coughed, ducking and weaving as if trying to ward off a swarm of bees. He had to be silenced.

Alessia picked up the mace with both hands and swung with all her might at his forehead. It made a sickening crunch as it connected and he dropped like a stone, his skull partially crushed inward.

Alessia surveyed her surroundings. The faint din of merriment emanated from the laneway to the street. The sound of boots clicking against the pavement moved up the lane toward her. Bianca and Livia. Alessia cleaned her sword on the tunic of the clubman as his life gurgled away.

With great care, she rearranged her dress and looked distastefully at the patches of dark blood from the stomach wound she'd inflicted on Mantoni. She retrieved the shoulder bag from where she was attacked first and drew out a light sleeveless gown which she threw over her head and pulled down to her ankles. With a practiced squeak, she called for her familiar to return to the bag. When the two women arrived, she was as well-groomed as if about to meet her beau, save for the cloth she was wiping on her blood-stained arm. Livia almost threw up and turned away, doubled over.

Bianca busied herself as they had agreed beforehand. She walked around the scene of the fight, shining her lantern inwards. Quite a spectacle for Livia to see on her first night out, but Alessia had no time now to take care of her. Two bloodied men, one very near death.

Bianca whispered to Alessia, "That poor man is choking; it'd be a mercy to give him a swift end."

Alessia looked back at Bianca, her face and manner already that of a noblewoman. "Then use the mace and make it quick," she said.

Bianca was taken aback. No doubt she thought Alessia was the best one to deliver the fatal blow. Her mouth closed into a pinched line, and she took the mace into her two hands, holding it away from her body. She inched ever slower towards the fallen man as though approaching the edge of a cliff. He grasped his throat.

"I'm sorry, Master," Bianca said. "It is your time." One blow ended his struggles, and Bianca turned to the other two, hanging her head.

She was doing well. Alessia moved slightly so she could see past Bianca to where Livia was recovering, and more importantly, to the laneway and the back of the Tavern. The man with the knife was still stretched out. Bianca looked over at Alessia, who shook her head and gestured for Bianca to move on to Maltoni. Bianca hesitated a little in front of him; his groans and movements were now beyond his control. After a little shiver, she once again hefted the mace.

Once the grisly business was done, Bianca recovered the curved dagger and put it in her basket, then searched the area with her lantern pointing inwards. There was just the headdress to be recovered. She knelt to pick it up, checking under the cauls for any damage to the wickerwork underneath. Alessia couldn't resist coming over to look for herself; she took it from Bianca and planted a kiss on the back of it. Bianca put it carefully in the basket and stooped to pick up a bloodied cloth. Voices approached. Alessia hissed at her to close the lantern and looked down at the ground.

Livia had been unable to help and kept well away while trying to not to get sick. Her arms were still clasped across her stomach when she saw a couple approaching from the lane. Her white face was an unwelcome sight to them; clearly they were looking for somewhere they wouldn't be disturbed. Livia turned and made a loud retching noise, but nothing came forth. She surreptitiously took the jug of wine from her shoulder bag, uncorked it and spilled some onto the ground to simulate vomit. She retched again, and turned around, wiping her mouth. The couple looked at her in disgust, then at the scene in the shadows behind; bodies on the ground, and two other women swaying unsteadily. They hurried away. Livia looked back at Alessia, who mimed applause. There was still enough wine left to spill on the bodies of the men to leave them reeking, but not enough to fill their own tumblers before they returned to the waiting carriage.

Alessia threw her bag and sword on the back seat so Bianca and Livia had to sit together on the other side. As she arranged the long gown to sit more comfortably, she felt Stolie wanting to come out from his pouch in the shoulder bag. She briefly looked over at the two women and decided it was time they met her familiar, so she coaxed him out into her cupped hands. Bianca shrieked and pressed herself back into the corner of the carriage, throwing one arm out protectively to cover Livia. Alessia ignored them both and made little squeaking noises to Stolie, stroking his sleek sides with her fingers. He bounced up her arms, drawing a gasp from Bianca, then sprawled across the back of her neck and peeked around at the two women.

"Oh, it's a stoat, Bianca, see its tail!" Livia looked from Stolie to Alessia and back again. "Does he bite?"

Alessia closed her eyes and smiled.

Mosquito Screens

By Finnbar Howell

The little body between them weighed almost nothing. As though all the brightness and life that had suffused her minutes before had real weight she was now relieved of. She seemed less real like this, Thomas thought. The blood pumping from her chest slowed, and he wanted to reach and stop it, to keep it inside of her. The bullet pierced Scarlett's heart, but he was unwilling to let this part of her slip away into the sawdust-covered floor.

The realization that their daughter was dead struck him like a physical blow. He was winded, unable to draw breath. Doubling over so his forehead rested against Rashad's chest, he gasped, and with each gasp he shuddered, and with each shudder Scarlett's body trembled in harmony. Rashad let out a low sound, a keening that rose in pitch and volume until he was wailing. He wrapped fingers into Thomas' hair and pressed him to his chest, and Thomas felt his scalp grown damp from the tears that poured down.

The tires retreated as swiftly as they advanced, and there had only been one shot. Perhaps it was meant as a warning, or to instill fear. Or perhaps the gunman had been aiming for Thomas or Rashad though the windows when the truck lurched in one of the ruts that dotted the ground around their dwelling. Either way, the bullet punched through the front door and the insect screen and found its resting place in a heart still owed a million beats.

They had neither of them seen the truck, nor the Tyce brothers, but there was no one else it could be. Thomas's head and heart had no room for rage yet. The world was still crumbling.

～

Thomas chuckled over his shoulder at the joke the old man who ran the general store made, and closed the door on his way out, careful to pull the insect screen tight. Mosquitos were out in force this summer, and it was worse down here in the town than up on the hill.

He packed the week's supplies into the panniers of his motorbike –a relic of his grandfather's brought from the old world that ran on actual petrol—and stood considering the pub, Twocrest Fortress. There were plenty of reasons to just start up and drive home. But hell, he helped build the Fortress. He spent three weeks in bed with broken ribs from catching the big central beam when it was falling on the workmen below. Thomas had as much right as any man to get himself a drink.

The Fortress was dim inside. A tallow candle burned gently in one corner, providing the only artificial light to add to the sunlight penetrating the dusty windows. Electric light fittings were set in strips into the ceiling, as well as the huge fireplace at one end of the room, but Daisy wasn't going to use those during the daytime for the three or so customers she'd get.

She nodded to Thomas as he entered; warmly, but warily too, with a little glance around to ensure none of the other patrons paid attention. They huddled around a game of dominos. None looked up as he entered.

Daisy was still his firm friend, but she had her bar to consider, her entire livelihood, and Thomas didn't blame her for her wariness. Rashad had been called out last month to treat an outbreak of Blue-Spot in a herd on the west side of town but had been sent for far too late. Half the herd was lost, and since then their reputation around the town, already tenuous at best, soured further. Especially when the town's other vet, Eric Tyce, claimed to any who'd listen that Rashad had been drunk and misdiagnosed the steers; that Eric himself could have saved them if he'd only been called instead.

The next day they'd pulled Scarlett out of the morning school she was only just getting used to when one of the other kids spit on her. She could be educated at home for a while. Rashad had plenty to teach her about animal care, and Thomas could show her how to fix machines like his Ma had showed him. He was actually looking forward to it.

"Alright, Daisy. Just some of your famous lemonade. No. I'll take a small beer as well."

"Will I just make you up a Radler?"

He shook his head "I like them separate."

He drank quietly, sitting at the bar and chatting quietly with Daisy about the waterfall over the ridge; whether she thought the town would be able to finish the dam before winter and if they'd have to pay for power when it was built. A few glances came from those around the domino table but no harsh words, only a half-hearted wave from a farmer whose generator Thomas had fixed last autumn.

Thomas heard the voices before the thud of boots on the porch.

Should he stay sitting to avoid confrontation, or stand so he wasn't low when they came in?

He started to get up, then went to sit again, half hovering by the stool as the door banged and the Tyce brothers strode in.

Eric was in front, as usual, taking off his wide-brimmed hat as he entered the room. Jimmy and Jake followed in his wake, neither bothering to remove their baseball caps.

"Well Daisy girl, would you ever put some light on in here so I can see your pretty face proper-" He stopped, standing in the middle of the room as he caught sight of Thomas.

Thomas returned fully to the stool and sipped his beer.

Eric approached in his peripheral vision, stopping beside him. "Surprised you've got the balls to come drinking in my watering hole."

"It's not yours, Eric. It's Daisy's, and I'm not looking for trouble."

"Well maybe you two bring that freak daughter of yours to another town and trouble won't be needed, will it?"

Thomas' grip tightened around the glass in his hand, but he did nothing beyond taking a quiet sip, of lemonade this time.

Eric knocked it from his hand, spilling the drink across his jeans and smashing the glass in the process.

"Look at me when I'm talkin' to you!"

Thomas grabbed Daisy's polishing rag from the bar and wiped his jeans as best he could. Then he picked up the other glass and drained his beer. "Thanks for the drinks Daisy. I must be running low on credit. You let me know if there's anything needs fixing about the place."

He stood, finding Eric's chin uncomfortably close to his eyes as he turned.

The big man looked down at him, all bulging shoulders and corded neck, the glint of primitive power visible around the irises. "If you and that dirty-skinned freak don't take your brat out of this place you'll end up just like that little whore who spawned—"

Thomas cut him off with a fist to his eye socket. Eric fell like a tree, straight over backwards and struck the wooden floor so hard the dominoes at the table nearby tumbled over.

Thomas stepped over him, straight past the other two gawking brothers, and out into the sunlight without looking back.

He tucked the knuckle dusters back into his coat pocket and started the bike.

There was no way that this wouldn't mean trouble, but they were equal to it. They'd handled worse before, he was sure of it.

~

Rain thundered onto the roof of the barn. The house's thatch was still unfinished, and they'd been living in here for half a year now. Thomas and Rashad had wanted to have the whole place finished for Iliza by the time she gave birth, but things kept cropping up—the sheep had broken out of their pen to scatter across the hills and half a week had been lost gathering them back up. Thomas spent three weeks in bed with broken ribs. The solar panels broke twice, and he didn't have the parts to fix them and had to improvise. So now, instead of a house, Iliza was lying on top of the towels that covered her bed in the barn, under the gentle glow of the infrared lamp.

Rashad said it shouldn't matter—it was warm and clean in here. What worried him was that her contractions were well under way, but neither the midwife nor the doctor had arrived. He stared out into the night from the side door, looking for any lights at all in the blackness. Thomas left Iliza's side for a moment and went over to lay a hand on his shoulder. "If they don't come, you can deliver it. I trust you. So does Iliza."

Rashad shook his head. "I don't have any drugs. All I have is for sheep since the drop never came through. On top of that my laser saw's on the fritz: if something goes wrong—"

"Nothing's going to go wrong. Have faith."

Rashad kissed him gently on the cheek, then turned back to the rain. "I just don't know why they haven't come."

Thomas hesitated. "In church, Brother Strous said we shouldn't have done it. He said a child with three parents is ungodly."

Rashad shook his head. "On the ship, it was almost common. Jesus, you'd think this place was the bloody cradle of civilization."

"Hey," Thomas said, turning Rashad away from the door. "Hey! I didn't say I think that. Come on. We'll be strong now. We'll be strong for the girls." *The girls*. It gave him a little trill.

They walked back to Iliza together. Rashad knelt down next to the bed and held her hand. "How are you feeling? Is there pressure? Pain?"

She looked up at him, blonde hair streaked across her face with sweat, green eyes slightly unfocused from the muscle relaxant he'd given her "Will the doctor be here soon? Something feels wrong."

~

The landing stage was crowded. Cranes and hovercrafts ferried cargo down from the bay of the ship where it stood, still cooling, dominating the landscape like a metal mountain. All-terrain vehicles set off in droves towards the hills to the south, while to the north packs of dogs pulled sleds—ill-suited to the rocky ground but invaluable on the snowy landscape at higher latitudes. A prison worker gang was already at work alongside a team of mules laying the railroad that would link the two first major settlements—Blue Skies and the ship itself, The Nebbersteller.

Rashad stopped to fish something out of his pack, barely off the ramp, and Thomas chided him with laughter in his voice. "First time breathing real air in your life and you're dragging your feet. Didn't you spend enough time with your notes and lists to organize a thousand bags?"

Rashad spoke without looking up. "First of all, anyone who thinks that air full of propulsion fumes is 'real' deserves a smack. I'll take the greenhouse deck any day. Second, fail to prepare, you prepare to fail, and third…" He looked up to meet Thomas' gaze and winked. "Third I can't think of anything so let's go get this goddamn bike you've been crowing about and hope you don't kill yourself the first time you use it outside of a simulator."

They walked side-by-side to the private vehicles depot, crossing muddy ruts and jumping ditches half full of water. The landing had really churned the ground up, and the rain turned the whole area into a quagmire. They dealt with unstable footing for the first time in their twenty-six years, and by the time they reached the depot both of them had muddy knees and sore elbows from falling.

The depot was a grand name for the hexagon marked out in brightly striped spray markings, with plastic tape for walls, flapping in the breeze. When they reached it, they found heard an argument in full swing.

The Cargo Master, a short, bald man with enormous calves visible between his boots and the bottom of his shorts, tapped a display pad angrily and shoved it toward a young woman with striking blonde hair who seemed vaguely familiar. She pushed the display aside. "I told you, it's not my fault your equipment is broken. I have a departure schedule, and if I don't get my horse today I miss my window and my colony will leave without me."

"Well, what the hell do you want me to do? Just let anyone come up and claim that anything is theirs? How do I know you're not a thief?" He squared up to her now, to Thomas' disbelief.

The girl didn't back down.

Thomas stepped past Rashad and tapped the Cargo Master on the shoulder. "Excuse me, sir. You may want to cool your head."

Rashad always said Thomas was too ready with his fists, and maybe he was, but this time it was the cargo master who threw a punch. Angry and fed up, breathing air with a higher nitrogen content than he was used to, the man felt the touch, heard the calm words and swung with a haymaker.

Thomas ducked under it and raised his arm to block the

inevitable blow from the other side. But the blow never landed.

The man laid face-down in the mud, arm twisted behind him with the wrist tucked under. All the girl had to do was lift gently and he squealed in undignified pain.

"Now. I could take that radio from your belt and report you for assault. Claim passenger's arrest or I suppose citizen's arrest now that we're on planet. But that would slow me down, and I just want my horse. So instead you're going to write a receipt on paper, which I will sign, and I will take my horse and go-"

"And my motorbike."

"And his motorbike. We'll take them and leave you be. Sound fair?"

That evening as they sat around their first non-electric fire, Thomas tried to place Iliza. She missed the departure of her colony after all and was considering whether to chase after them the next morning or just set off on her own. It seemed to be a popular notion. Hell, it was what Thomas and Rashad were doing.

"I never really liked them much anyway. I wanted to go and settle with the other girls from the team, but we were split up by mandate, for genetic reasons apparently."

Rashad snapped his fingers with a grin. "I know where I know you from now."

~

Rashad was faster than him and tore away down the long curve of the metal corridor. The shouts receded behind them as they passed a 3D poster for one of the big fight nights coming up; champion Sherrie Taylor vs. challenger Iliza Winters.

It was Thomas' twenty-third birthday, and for a treat Rashad snuck him into the engine ring, stealing rad suits and paying his brother to re-program their access chips for the day. Thomas had been in heaven. Until they got caught.

They'd been on one of the huge circular walkways that ringed the ship. Far enough from the outer skin that the centrifugal force that simulated gravity would probably kill them if they fell. Thomas laid flat, the metal grill of the walkway pressing into his shoulder blades, watching the rotating piston that controlled the air lock pumps spin huge and majestic under the never-ceasing force of hydrogen fusion. This was the final stop on their tour. They'd already climbed up into the bowels of rotational control, looked down into the workings of a guidance thruster half dismantled for repair, and snuck on hands and knees past the guards at life support systems.

There was no radiation danger here, and their helmets and

gloves lay a meter or so away. Rashad's hands had grown rough from the countless hours he spent training with the small portion of the ship's livestock kept out of cryo, and as he absently stroked the back of it, Thomas noticed the hair growing there was getting thicker. He said it to Rashad.

"Expect a whole lot more where that came from, boy. Indian men are always hairy."

Thomas tugged at the hair playfully. "Do you think we'll have that again?"

"What?"

"Countries and borders and stuff. On planet?"

"Doubt it. Only, what, ten percent of people weren't born on ship? And a lot of that older generation will be gone in another few years." Rashad winced. "Sorry. I know your babcia just died. But I doubt anyone's going to go back to Earth ways. We've all learned the spacer way together. One big community spread out over a whole planet."

"It's going to be beautiful. Perfect."

"I hope so. People are funny though."

Thomas was going to ask him what he meant when they heard shouting and the shriek of a whistle coming from a few hundred meters down the walkway.

Rashad froze in place, face a comical mask of shock until Thomas grabbed him by the collar and hauled him up. They dashed along, boots clanking the mesh until they reached a ladder and climbed two hundred meters back to the central rings and passenger bays of the ship. Less than halfway up Thomas felt another resonance in the metal as someone else mounted the bottom.

"Come on, faster!" Rashad urged him from below.

Up through the hatchway, which they closed firmly and wedged with a nearby fire extinguished, they could still faintly hear the whistle blasting through the thick hatch as they ran, laughing, down the hall.

⌒

Thomas felt Rashad's soft hand on his shoulder as he sat on the edge of the bed. "Why are you so tense? It's okay."

Thomas brushed his hand away, didn't look around. "Theresa."

There was a long pause. Thomas could picture Rashad gathering his thoughts in that quiet way he did when he was going to say something important. Thomas' cabin smelled strongly of their sex; a sweet, gentle smell completely different to the smell Theresa made when she snuck away from her family quarters late at night to join him.

"Well. It was my fault. I knew you were taken. I shouldn't have started this. I'll tell her it's not your fault."

Thomas shook his head. "That's insane. I've been seeing her since I was fourteen, that's nearly three years. Even if I did think it was your fault at all, I couldn't not tell her myself. She's so good, Rash, she's a good person. I just can't bring myself to—"

"Then I'll…" Rashad paused again, and Thomas could hear the strain in his voice. "I'll leave. I won't contact you anymore, and you can stay with her. You guys can be happy together and I'll… I have my Vet entry trial next month, and I'm sure I'll get in. I'll be fine."

Thomas didn't know what he would have said at that moment. Part of him desperately wanted to tell him *no. Don't go. I'll be strong. I'll do what I need to.* But the other part couldn't bear the hurt on Theresa's face.

Either way, the choice was taken away as the door gave its three-second proximity bleep: someone with access was approaching his door.

He stood, grabbed the blanket to throw it over Rashad, but it caught on his foot.

The door slid open, and Theresa bounded in shouting. "I've got a surprise for—"

She stopped stock still just inside the door in a short skirt and a skimpy rad-bed bikini, the words *Sto Lat!* were spelled out in glitter across her stomach.

The only thing Thomas could think was, *It doesn't work for happy birthday outside of the song. If she spoke Polish, she'd know that.*

~

It was cold the day Thomas turned seven. One of the three temperature regulators on their ring, Ring 12, had broken down, and until the engineers could design and print the broken part, the whole ring was five degrees Kelvin below normal.

To Thomas, who had never been out of the carefully regulated central passenger rings, it felt like he might die.

Not so bad at the party, but when the other kids left and Thomas helped carefully collect the detritus for re-purposing, he crawled into the bed in his cabin, under the blankets, and refused to come out until his babcia, his grandmother, arrived.

She was clad, as usual, in her faded light blue cardigan with the missing button at the top, and she had a very special present for him.

Because growing room in the Nebberstellar was at a premium, luxury crops like sugar were beyond expensive. His babcia must have saved for weeks to afford the powdered sugar donut she gave him. It was wrapped up in a delicate little cloth and spongy to the touch, almost pulsating with the jam inside.

She watched as he ate it, savoring every mouthful while still making sure to eat no more than half so he could offer everyone in the family a little bit.

When he'd finished his hands and arms were dusted with powdered sugar, which he proceeded to lap off.

She laughed when she saw this. "Jesteś Kotem Tomaszc?" *Are you a cat Tomaszc?*

He stood up indignantly. "Jestem Chlopcy Babcia!" *I am a boy!* "And my name is Thomas!"

"Don't be angry with me," she said, pulling him into her lap. "My Tomaszc, my little kot. My handsome grandson." She pinched his cheek. "Oh, you will break hearts. You will break so many hearts."

THE ELIXIR MEN

BY JACK DOWD

Katie staggered through the shop door, fighting the urge to vomit. Harriet fished her mobile out of her pocket complaining about the lack of signal while a display case holding what seemed to be a variety of peacock feathers entranced Sean. Other display cases hosting unusual items dotted the shop: a wooden mannequin on strings, a necklace decorated with runes, extinguished candles on coffee tables placed next to sunken settees.

"What is this place?" Katie asked. Bile burnt the back of her throat. She caught a whiff of incense as she passed by a candle.

"Occult shop," Sean answered pulling a book off a shelf and inspecting the cover. "Y' know? Black magic and all that. Druids, Celts, Native Indians." Katie noticed that Sean's glasses were askew and his clothes tattered.

"Uber is on the way. It's right around the corner," Harriet said. Blood dripped down the scratch on her cheek as she glanced at the displays with disinterest.

Katie caught sight of her reflection in a display case. Blue mascara ran down her cheeks and her handbag dangled from her arm, half unzipped. She collapsed onto a settee, grimacing as her clothes stuck to her, like a second skin. A blue tear drop bottle rested on the table next to her. Katie shook the container and watched the sapphire liquid swirl.

"I don't think that's water," Sean said.

"No, it isn't." A shop keeper appeared behind the counter holding a steaming tin kettle. Katie hadn't heard him enter. "Are you three alright? Were you attacked?"

"Nah," Harriet said, "we just had a rough night, right Kat?"

"Yeah," Katie muttered.

"Do you want me to make you a cup of tea while you order a taxi?" the shop keeper asked. "The kettle's just boiled." Katie couldn't avert her gaze from his. His eyes were mismatched, the left was brown and the right green. His eyebrows were gray, yet his hair was dyed jet black.

Katie shrugged. "How long have you been open? I haven't been in here before."

"Are you local?" the shopkeeper asked.

"We go to the Uni just around the corner," Sean said, "but we don't want to walk it in this rain."

The shop keeper nodded and poured the contents of the kettle, green tea Katie suspected, into three china cups. "What you have there is called the Elixir of Desire. Once you have taken a draught, you will obtain whatever your heart wants the most."

Harriet rolled her eyes. Sean lost interest and looked out at the rain for the approaching Uber.

"If it helps me forgot about bloody Kenneth then fine," Katie scoffed. "How much?"

"You're not actually going to buy that, are you?" Harriet asked.

"How much?"

"For you, not a penny. Think of it as compensation for a bad night."

"There you go." Katie picked up the vial and took the offered receipt. "It's free."

Sean opened the shop door causing the bell to tinkle. "Uber's here. C'mon."

Harriet grabbed Katie's hand and dragged her toward the door. Katie allowed Harriet to snatch the receipt and cradled the bottle as though it were a child.

"Thank you," Katie shouted to the man as Harriet pulled her into the rain. As they clambered into the Uber and told the driver they planned on splitting the bill three ways, Katie caught a glimpse of the shop front. Grey letters above the door frame read *The Elixir Men.*

~

When the buzzing jolted her awake, Katie couldn't understand what caused the noise. Or why her head hurt. She extracted her hand from the bed sheets, reached for her phone, and pressed snooze. Then she remembered why her head hurt.

The memory of the previous night returned to her in snapshots. Arriving at the nightclub, shots of tequila at the bar, dancing, Kenneth kissing another girl, crying with Harriet outside, Harriet trying to claw Kenneth's eyes out, leaving in the rain with Sean and Harriet, the strange shop on the way home…

Her phone vibrated again. Katie squinted at the screen.

History Lecture alarm. 08:45.

She swore and became aware of how cold her bed was without a second body.

Why did Kenneth kiss that girl? What's wrong with me?

Summoning her strength, Katie pushed away the covers and stumbled out of her room and down the corridor to the shared bathroom. Sean and Harriet's door was closed, but Katie thought she heard movement.

When she returned to her room after brushing her teeth, Katie noticed a blue bottle on her makeup drawer. Her thoughts were sluggish and slow to form. Hadn't it been in the occult shop? She tried to remember, but the image of Kenneth kissing the other girl burned with intensity.

I wish I could forget all about him.

She sniffed the liquid and then sampled a drop. The tang convinced Katie it was not drinking water.

~

"Heard from Kenneth yet?" Harriet asked as Katie took her seat and the lecture hall lights dimmed. The screen of the interactive whiteboard glared in the gloom.

"Huh?" Katie winced as Dr. Cole started his lecture in that signature monotone his students loathed him for. Katie was thankful for the dark. She hadn't had time to apply her make up.

"Have you heard from Kenneth?"

"No…"

Harriet scoffed. "Typical man."

Katie opened her mouth, but no words came. A pang of dread and depression struck when she heard that name, but she didn't know why.

"You look seriously hung over," Harriet said as the Dr. Cole changed the PowerPoint slide.

"Yeah, I feel it." She scribbled down the dates of the Cuban missile crisis displayed on the board.

"Do you know how much you had to drink?"

Katie shook her head. A mistake that further agitated her headache.

"He's not put anything on his Facebook wall," Harriet said glancing at her phone under the table.

"Who?"

Harriet stared at her. "Kenneth."

"Who's Kenneth?"

"Oh, we're blanking him now?" Harriet smirked.

Katie didn't answer. Something was wrong. Something was very wrong. She sat throughout the rest of the lecture in silence.

~

Sean heard the girls returning through his open door.

"Everything okay?" he shouted down the corridor. When he didn't receive an answer, he followed the source of the noise into Katie's room.

Katie clutched her desk for support, face pale.

"What happened?" Sean asked from the doorway.

"Kat's not feeling well," Harriet said. "Sit down on your bed, dear."

"Sore head?" Sean stepped into the cramped bedroom. He spotted a blue bottle on Katie's desk.

Katie muttered a response and clambered onto her mattress.

"We're going to leave you to sleep it off, okay?" Harriet said waving Sean toward the door. Sean nodded, picked up the bottle, and stepped into the corridor. Harriet closed the door behind them.

"She's heartbroken, isn't she?" Sean asked. He thought he could hear Katie crying through the door.

"I think she's ill," Harriet said. "She doesn't want to think about Kenneth. It's like a mental block."

"She'll get better, won't she?"

"Yeah," Harriet said, "but she needs time to sleep. What's that you've got?" Harriet asked nodding to bottle. "And where the hell were you this morning?"

"Yeah, I slept in. The PowerPoint is probably online anyway."

"Whatever, you should have been in class."

Sean rolled his eyes and returned to his room. The lecture notes weren't posted online yet, so he continued typing his overdue essay.

Sean tried to ignore the fear. The fear of what Dr. Cole would say. The fear of what Dad would say. The fear of failing.

He took a sip of the energy drink from Katie's room.

Yuk! You're losing it, man. You're losing it. I just wish I knew all this stuff.

Sean looked back at his laptop. What date did the Cuba missile crisis happen?

Nineteen…sixty two. That was it. October… Sixteenth to twenty-eighth.

Sean glanced at the clock on his laptop as he started his introductory paragraph. 13:21. When he completed the essay, the clock read 13:40.

He looked at his twelve-page essay. He didn't feel the sense of indifference he felt with most of his essays. In fact, Sean thought it was his best essay so far.

He opened Facebook. Kenneth had changed his relationship status from "It's complicated" to "in a relationship."

Kat will go mad when she sees this.

He scrolled down his news feed to see an old school friend

shared the results of a psychological quiz that deemed his friend a psychopath.

That's wrong. Psychopaths don't understand the difference between right and wrong. Sociopaths do, but they just don't care… How do I know that?

Sean scrolled down.

Quiz: How many of these historical events do you know?

Sean accepted the challenge. Two minutes later his laptop screen read:

100%. Wow. Top of the class. Why don't you share your results with your friends?

Sean laughed and pressed share. He didn't know what year the Spanish Armada had failed or who had been killed at the start of World War One until he saw the question. The answers materialized in his mind.

Sean grimaced and turned off his laptop.

Headaches are caused by the overuse of structures in the brain that are pain sensitive, such as the dorsal posterior insula, the sensory strip and … What?

He sat down on his bed and tried to think about the calming meditation exercises he remembered being taught in school.

The first recorded use of meditation is linked to the Hindu religion and is dated around 1500 BCE. Meditation was popularized in Japan in the year 653 when the monk Dosho returned from China and opened a meditation hall in Japan.

Stop!

The stop sign was first created in Michigan 1915 and was standardized in 1922 for the rest of America.

Sean's headache turned into a migraine.

⁓

"Are you two coming out tonight?" Harriet shouted down the corridor. She brushed over her scratch until it was concealed under her makeup. Sean's door was half open. Harriet pushed it aside to find Sean typing on his laptop.

"Catching up on coursework?" she asked, bemused, but her smile faltered when Sean turned to her. Both his eyes were bloodshot.

"Yeah. I've got so much work to do." His voice sounded distant, as though focusing on something else.

Harriet picked up the blue bottle by his desk. "Okay… but no more alcohol?"

Sean didn't answer her. Harriet closed his door and tried to ignore the unease building inside her.

He's gonna burn himself out if he's not careful.

Pausing to listen for the sound of sobbing, Harriet knocked on

Katie's door.

"Come in."

Harriet opened the door. Katie was cocooned in her bed.

"How you feeling, girl?" Harriet tried not to look at the strewn clothes littering the floor.

Katie shrugged. "I'm not coming out tonight."

"You could probably find another boy at the bar," Harriet suggested.

"Why would I need another man?" Katie asked.

Harriet half smiled. "You best get some sleep, yeah? I'm going to grab my bag then I'll be off." She took a swig from the wine bottle grimaced at the taste and left.

~

Harriet examined herself in the club's bathroom mirror. She reapplied her lipstick, a bright shade of red that helped earn her free drinks at the bar. She'd lost count of the amount of chat up lines she'd heard and was thankful for the privacy of the bathroom.

Still looking good, she decided. *Shame it couldn't be like this last night.*

Music flooded into the bathroom as the door swung open and two girls staggered in. Harriet glanced up at them in the mirror. Both were drunk, and one had a broken heel.

Harriet gave them a polite smile. *A couple more songs till the next club,* she decided. She was about to run a comb through her hair when she noticed the girls staring at her from the doorway.

"Alright?" Harriet asked.

"You're beautiful," the girl with the broken heel said.

"Um...thanks?" She could smell the alcohol on their breath.

The girl hobbled forward, but her friend knocked her onto the floor.

"Oh, my god." Harriet stepped towards the fallen girl but the second girl stood between them. She reached out and ran her hand through Harriet's hair.

"What are you doing?"

"I just want to touch it," the girl said with no hint of remorse.

Harriet pushed her away and sprinted for the door only to find her way blocked by a man, leering at her.

"This is the girl's toilet," the girl with the broken heel shouted using a hand dryer to steady herself, but the boy in the doorway didn't listen. Harriet shouldered past him and ran onto the dance floor.

The crowd seemed to have tripled. Harriet forged a path toward the exit, deafened by the pounding music and disorientated by the throng of bobbing people and flashing lights.

"Alright?" the security guard asked, as she reached the door.

"No, I—" Harriet pointed into the crowd and screamed as those nearest took a step toward her.

"Help me," she pleaded, but the guard smirked and rolled up his sleeves to reveal his biceps.

"Oi, I saw her first." A fist flung out of the crowd and collided with the guard's cheek. Harriet screamed as the guard's blood splattered down her dress.

The guard snarled and lunged into the crowd.

Harriet fled.

When she was several streets away from the club, Harriet stopped running. She leaned against the wall of a café to catch her breath.

What the hell was that?

A car drove past and the occupants jeered and cat-called. Harriet ignored them and watched her breath mist.

I'm going home.

She fished her phone out of her handbag to call an Uber and noticed something white crumpled at the bottom of her bag.

～

The Elixir Men. Refund available upon request.

Katie read the receipt and looked up at the shop. The gray letters reading The Elixir Men were familiar. "I don't remember it," she said.

Sean examined the stonework. "This building is at least fifty years old," he declared. He said it so confidently Katie didn't doubt him. "Have either of you two seen it before?"

Katie shook her head and looked at Harriet who said goodbye to the Uber driver.

"He said he drives up and down this road most days," Harriet said as the driver pulled away. "He was certain he hasn't seen the shop before. He swears it's new."

"That's impossible," Sean said.

As Sean and Harriet argued, Katie knocked on the shop door. It opened immediately.

"Can I help you?" the man before them asked.

Katie looked at the man's mismatched eyes. They masked any sign of recognition.

"Yeah, we'd like to return this please," Katie held out the bottle. The man took the vial, peered at the contents, and asked, "Do you have a receipt?"

Katie held out the scrap of paper.

"I see. I hope you've all learned something."

"What do you mean?" Katie asked, but the door was closed.

The first thing Katie noticed was her vibrating phone. She jolted awake and realized this wasn't her bedroom. She sat on a bench at the side of the road, next to Sean and Harriet who both stirred.

"Where are –" Katie began to ask, but she recognized the street. "Were we here last night?"

An abandoned shop on the opposite side of the road showed no markings or signs of what it once may have been, but it was evident it had been derelict for a long time.

"Did we go drinking again?" she asked.

"No idea," Sean answered. "I guess so." He stood up and stretched. "Man, we shouldn't have had a night out. We've got too much revision to do."

"Yeah…" Harriet muttered. "I'm not drinking again. Ever. That your phone, Kat?"

Katie fished the phone out of her pocket. *Kenneth calling.*

She pressed ignore.

Leon Strange

By Trent L Cannon

Some days it doesn't pay to get out of bed.

The thought rang through my head as I stumbled to my feet. I said rang because that was the noise the thought had to compete with. My hand pressed against something rough and stone as I dragged myself to my feet, clinging to it for dear life as I struggled to make sense of my surroundings.

I'd been running through a closed park, sneaking through the opening in the tall fence along the River Ouse that is usually used by teenagers looking to be just rebellious enough to impress their friends. I used the path because it was a quicker way through town. If I was late to date night one more time, Sarah would either end me or our relationship. Sometimes it was tough to tell which. Besides, there were worse places in York to rush through than the Museum Gardens. It overflowed with a mixture of nature and history that always had a new surprise.

Some days more than others.

"I must suggest that you flee. You will only distract me."

Accidental poetry aside, the woman's voice shook some of the cobwebs clear from my head. I lifted my gaze from my feet. I'd wandered around the corner of a stone structure, left over from either Roman or Medieval times, hearing a woman shout, expecting to find the victim of a broken heel on the cobblestones or someone startled by some geese walking around like they own the place. Both are perfectly valid things to find on a warm evening in York.

Big, green, and frighteningly strong, I hadn't been expecting. The thing in front of me looked like something out of a nightmare, with its too-long arms and too-broad face filled with a bulbous, crooked nose and mouth full of broken teeth. It loomed over me and the rest of the gardens, a giant in a world two sizes too small. I wanted to check behind me, to see if the park was still there, but I didn't dare take my eyes off it.

Then it moved, and I realized the real danger of this thing wasn't its strength or size. Before I could flinch, it closed the distance between itself and the woman, slamming an open hand into her side before she could get out of the way. She grunted, stifling the kind of shout that had summoned me, and crumbled to the ground, rolling several feet before settling face down on the grass.

Nothing that size should be able to move so fast. I took a step backward, in the only direction that made any sense. It started to lumber toward her, half stalking and half skulking forward. She began to climb to her feet and only made it to a knee, but it didn't seem to bother her. Despite the wall of green and gruesome towering over her, this little blond woman, who clutched something around her neck in a tight fist, somehow managed to appear more frightening.

I found my feet beneath me and took a step forward. It didn't seem right to make her do all the hard work and face all the danger. Maybe I was mistaken, but if I could at least distract the thing for a second, maybe we could both escape. Besides, how tough could this thing be?

The gardens were filled with remains of civilizations dating back to the Romans, who had occupied the city, scattered among the trees and winding stone paths. I couldn't remember what most used to be, but I did spot a fair-sized piece on the ground next to me. I picked it up. A thousand years of history as a weapon in my hand. I hurled the stone at the monster.

It hit with a loud thud that sounded impressive, but, judging by how slowly and casually the creature turned toward me, didn't accomplish much. It did, however, get its attention, which was something I convinced myself a few moments earlier was a good thing. I doubted my strategy as its red eyes stared at me. No malice or anger. Just a cold, distant emptiness.

I desperately wished for a plan. Instead, I took an inventory of my options. I was alone, weaponless, against something I wasn't sure any weapon could hurt. It was bigger, stronger, and faster than me.

The creature took a step toward me. I bolted as fast as I could to try to get away.

Funny thing about York. It was built on top of older York. The Normans built over what the Vikings built over the Romans. I ran toward some tall stone pillars jutting out of the ground ahead as heavy footsteps gained from behind. Gaps between the pillars remained and, I hoped, would be narrow enough for me to hide behind.

I didn't turn. I ran track as a kid and knew never to look, or it would cost the race. More important, I did not, under any circumstances, want to know how close that thing was to me.

I reached the gap as something big, flat, and heavy hit me in the back. It would leave a horrendous bruise, but the force of it pushed me through the gap and onto the ground on the other side. I scrambled to my feet, thankful they still worked. The gap between the stone structures was only around three feet wide, more than enough for me but this thing was having real difficulty trying to squeeze through to catch me. And it had helpfully pushed me forward and just out of its reach.

I panted, letting out a breath of relief. A long, clawed arm strained and struggled for me, coming uncomfortably close to grabbing my foot until I pulled it away. I leaned back onto my hands, propped up on the grass as I watched it reach for me in vain. I even managed a relieved smile as I caught my breath.

Until its shoulder slipped through the gap and it looked just a few seconds away from shoving its way through.

"Oh, come on," I complained as I dragged myself to my feet.

I'm not necessarily fast when it comes to running, but, with something like that clawing at me, I managed to move damn quick. If I'd been smart, I would have waited for another second or two, until it reached my side, before fleeing through the gap to its left and running back where I came. Unfortunately, I didn't go into this with a plan, and I wasn't about to make one now. I bolted back to the woman, still kneeling and panting, but better.

"Come on, we need to get out of here." I picked her up by her arm, trying to drag her to her feet. She was heavier than she looked, but she managed to stand.

"You should run, but I will stay," she said with surprising force. "I won't let it get away."

As she spoke, her necklace began to glow. A faint light pulsed outward from the small ring hanging from the metal chain.

"What is it?" I asked, pointing to the thing that was rapidly dislodging itself from the ruins.

"A troll," she answered. The fact that she said it didn't bother me. But she said it so casually.

I started to argue but stopped myself. The woman with the glowing necklace probably knew better than I did.

"Right," I nodded. It roared and pulled as hard as it could. The pillars shook. The troll nearly tore down something that survived almost a thousand years of wind, rain, and human ingenuity. "Can you actually beat it?"

"Given time to focus my spell," she said, her voice already distant and her necklace pulsing brighter. "I can unleash the fires of Hell."

Under the circumstances, I didn't question the fact that she talked about magic. I certainly didn't want to draw attention to the fact that she rhymed when she spoke. I didn't even want to consider if she was using colorful language when she talked about hellfire.

"I'll see if I can keep its attention," I said, sounding far more sure than I felt as I put distance between her and me.

The troll pulled itself free and turned to find me. Or anyone. It didn't look picky.

It charged at me, ignoring the woman in favor of a closer target. Which was probably for the best; it saved me the trouble of trying to figure out how to draw its attention. Instead, I did what worked well for me up to that point.

I ran, but this time I tried to use at least a bit of a method.

I ran toward it for as long as my nerve held, which wasn't as long as I would like to admit. A second passed. Another. The heavy *thump thump thump* of its footsteps drew close. When my nerve broke, I changed direction as quick as I could and said a silent prayer to any god who would listen that this thing played by the same rules as everyone else.

Air brushed against me as it swung a huge hand out, but, after it passed, I was still breathing and on my feet. A glance backward revealed it stumbling away from me, struggling to change direction as I did.

I slowed down and watched. It was big, heavy, and surprisingly fast, but that only meant it took a lot longer to change direction. It was the only advantage I had over it, so I was damn well going to exploit it. If this thing was as brainless as it seemed, I might just get out of this alive.

The troll stopped and stared at me, the same way I stared at it. I expected it to charge and try the same thing, like a big dumb animal. Instead, it reached down and grabbed a chunk of dirt as big as me and wretched for a moment. The muscles in its arms visibly strained under green skin.

In the time it took to figure out what it was doing, the troll pulled a chunk of earth up and pitched it at me. All I could do was turn and take it on my side instead of my face.

The world darkened for an instant, like a bad edit in my memory. When I opened my eyes, the troll stood over me, reaching for me with clawed hands outstretched. Its mouth widened, full of crooked, yellow teeth.

I didn't have room to run, and my body hurt too much to fight back. So I did the only thing that made sense.

I shut my eyes and waited for what came next.

A moment passed, and nothing happened. I briefly wondered if this thing played with its food, but I pushed the thought aside and filed it under "Not Helping."

Another moment passed. I wasn't dead yet.

A flash of light so bright that, if my eyes hadn't been closed,

I'd be blind. Instead, it stunned me, and I turned my head away, rubbing until the spots in front of me disappeared.

When I opened my eyes, the troll vanished. The blond woman stood beside me, the light from her necklace fading.

Monsters. Magic. This whole night was unreal.

The woman dropped to her knees, panting and gasping for air. I didn't know how much effort it took to kill something the size of a shed, but it seemed like a lot. She watched me for a second and, satisfied that I would survive, fell back onto the soft ground beside me. We lay there, our arms stretched out at our sides as we both took a moment to savor the fact we had survived. Eventually, our breathing slowed from loud gasps to mere panting and we managed to speak

"You have questions," she said in a tone that didn't suggest she wanted to answer them.

"Just a few," I admitted. I turned my head to look at her, but she stared straight up at the night sky.

"The answers are dangerous."

"The best ones are."

"You are taking this surprisingly well," she said, turning her head to look at me. Hard, cold blue eyes pierced into me, making it hard to discern if she looked at me or through me.

I considered her comment. I spent my childhood with my head buried in books, comics, and video games. I watched every sci-fi and fantasy movie I could find. All of them far beyond the realm of reality. Yet, part of me always wished they weren't. That I'd wake up one morning and find something just beyond reality.

"I guess so," I said, cracking a small smile. "Maybe I hit my head harder than I think, but I've also spent most of my life in a fantasy world. Heck, I've daydreamed weirder stuff than that before."

The park fell silent. People would ask questions in the morning when they unlocked the gates, and some very undeserving group would get the blame for it, but that seemed like the perfect problem to leave for the morning. Or, if possible, to avoid entirely.

I forced myself to sit up, hugging my knees to my chest for support as I breathed in the cooling air. What do you say to a woman who has enough power to make a monster go from tower of gruesome muscle to nothing in a matter of seconds?

The only thing that is important, I suppose.

"I'm Leon, by the way," I said, extending my hand to her.

"Marianne," she said, turning onto her side and taking my hand. "And your life is about to become very strange."

Then she did something I didn't expect.

She smiled back at me.

"There isn't any going back from this, you know," she warned me, her grip tightening. "Once your eyes are opened to the way the world really is, you can't close them again."

I was bruised, battered, and didn't know how to explain all of this to Sarah. She had a far lower threshold for my nonsense lately, and she wasn't going to accept the old "a troll made me late" excuse. Still, that didn't seem important at that moment. As scary as it had been, the part of me that always hoped the world was weirder than it seemed was desperate to see just how weird it could get.

"Count me in," I nodded. "Let's see what's out there."

"Good," she said, her eyes alight with a mischievous energy. "Because trolls usually come in pairs, so we need to go find number two."

"Wait, there's more?" I coughed, the ball of excitement in my stomach turning to regret. "I thought we were done."

Marianne laughed and climbed to her feet, dragging me with her.

She wasn't wrong, of course. My life was becoming very strange.

THE MINCER

BY D.J. VANDERSTADT

The first call from Dispatch came in at around 8 p.m. Stench levels reached a critical Phase.

Meyer and DeBock were on duty in the Control Room. The unwelcome call interrupted a marathon game of Banzai. Both men were notorious gamblers and not easy to distract when on a roll.

DeBock, in particular, was a well-known visitor of illegal events organized by the syndicates.

Despite the fact that he was a crafty player, he had a habit of overplaying even the best of hands. As a result, DeBock was up to his neck in financial problems. At regular intervals, merciless enforcers showed up on his doorstep demanding substantial collections. Recent threats involving severe bodily harm had forced him into hiding. His credit finally ran out.

Every time DeBock was about to win a hand at the tables, his powerful opponents doubled up the bet. DeBock reached the point where even the lowest stakes exceeded his modest resources.

Meyer, on the contrary, recently struck real gold. A distant relative passed away. To his surprise, he received a sizeable sum of money. That day Meyer had just visited the bank. Now, a duffel-bag with wads of sweet cash sat at the bottom of his locker. But Meyer being Meyer, simply had to share his secret with someone. When DeBock laid eyes on what was in the bag, his mind immediately went into overdrive. He was determined to syphon off some of the content. The fact that Meyer was unattentive to detail in games came as a bonus. He simply missed the ability to bluff his way through life. It made him like putty in the hands of his opponent.

That night the Wheel of Fortune turned clearly in Meyer's favor. To DeBock's chagrin, his colleague won hand after hand. But, as the night wore on that would change. By the time the second call came in, DeBock had already pulled back a couple of games.

In Zone B, a critical situation rapidly ensued. But it wasn't until the third call that the men reluctantly broke off their game. Meyer went over to the control panel.

"No shit!" he cried. "Hey DeBock come over for a sec, what do you make of this?"

DeBock, Banzai straws still in hand, squinted at the row of indicators. Judged by the gauges on the panel a firm plan of action was required. "Bloody hell!" he cussed. "That's a potential Phase Red."

Meyer grunted. "Now we're seriously screwed."

DeBock spat on the floor. Shifts like these made him loathe his dead-end job more than anything.

Both men stared at the radio transmitter in somber anticipation.

A minute or so later Dispatch came on the air.

Meyer took the call.

~

Earlier that night, a Deep Sonar Probe detected abnormally high concentrations of Methane and Hydrogen in Zone B.

This meant there was a serious health risk for the surrounding areas. Zone B had quite a fierce reputation because of the slaughterhouses in the area. Meyer prayed in silence that it wasn't The Mincer they were probing.

The Mincer was a notorious black spot where people disappeared without a trace. Its treacherous reputation was more than once confirmed by graphic first-hand accounts from senior staff members. A Patrol Unit, long since dissolved, once lost three men in six months. Their bodies were never found, but some pieces of equipment had washed ashore on the banks of a Drainage Canal at the outskirts of the city. Of that ill-fated Unit, DeBock happened to be the last member still on active duty. Rumour had it that at the bottom of the Mincer mutated life forms had spontaneously developed.

Meyer and DeBock heard the H2S alarm going off from inside the locker-room. A red light above the airlock started flashing. They put on HAZMAT suits and breathing apparatus in silence. As a standard procedure, they assisted each other with the final adjustments to masks and bottles of compressed air. Minutes later they headed to the hazard zone.

DeBock steered the rubber dinghy with a steady hand through a maze of narrow canals. The underground river that once gave the city its name now functioned as its main sewer. Some of the brick catacombs dated back to the Napoleonic era.

From the high vaults, chutes released a torrent of raw sewage into the canals below. Rats the size of rabbits hid between the brickwork. In the glare of the magnesium lamps, their fat pink tails whipped up the murky waters of the canal. Above their heads, cast iron manhole-covers blotted out the bright light that flooded the city's boulevards at night.

DeBock knew the sewer system like the back of his hand. He only checked the rusty directional signs now and then, just to be sure.

Despite his protective gear, Meyer's stomach wrenched when imagining the filth and stench out there. He often contemplated a career change. The money he kept in his locker offered a new future. He might even retire, maybe first go to Las Vegas or Macao...

Suddenly an incoming message over the radio made the men startle. Meyer almost dropped the receiver. With a shaky voice, he responded, "Yeah Meyer... Unit 7 here... Come in Dispatch..."

The Dispatcher on the other end floated in and out on waves of static. His fragmented message confirmed Meyer's worst fear. Flow-Control had finished analyzing the DSP data.

Dispatch officially declared Zone B a hazard zone, giving it a Code Red.

After a curt 'roger that' Meyer flicked the switch with force.

DeBock, drowned out by the sound of the outboard, made a questioning gesture. Meyer simply gave him thumbs down. In response, the dinghy accelerated sharply, and the men were on their way for a confrontation with the Mincer.

Blockages in Zone B were notorious. They almost always required high-pressure flushing to be cleared away. The Mincer was a concrete elbow pipe with a diameter of two meters. Its shape caused the trouble. Twice a day a diagonal chute that gave out onto the center of the Mincer dumped tons of organic waste from the slaughterhouses above it. The flow consisted of half-digested chunks of meat and splintered bone. It had the nasty habit of piling onto the grid at the bottom of the Mincer.

De Bock checked his watch. He knew exactly what time the chute would start pumping. Dumps took place simultaneously with the passing of the last metro that ran through a tunnel alongside the Mincer. Time was short.

When the men arrived at the spot, all detectors went crazy. The digital readings of Methane CH_4, H_2S, and CO_2 were off the chart. DeBock cursed aloud. One of them had to go down the Mincer to place the probe. After they lifted the heavy manhole-cover onto its side, DeBock set a crowbar to keep it in an upright position. The opening barely allowed one man to squeeze through, let alone with a bottle of compressed air on his back. By using a flashlight, the men peered down into the Mincer. They could see all the way to where the chute bent. Neither of them showed any initiative to go down the slippery shaft. They avoided direct eye contact.

As always, it was DeBock who broke the stalemate. After all, there was nothing that couldn't be solved with a quick round of Banzai. From his breast pocket, he took two toothpicks of which he broke one in half. The idea was simple and straightforward, the person drawing the shortest straw would go down and install the probe.

Meyer, who had been winning all night, rose to the challenge. He felt invincible. "Bring it on," he jeered.

While DeBock brought it, he observed Meyer's every move. He also witnessed how the smugness on Meyer's face gave way to disbelief when he discovered the broken toothpick in the palm of his glove.

Before Meyer went down, DeBock attached a rope to his safety harness. The radio transmitter stayed on the surface in case Dispatch contacted them with the latest data. Meyer slung the probe and hose for the pressure injector over his shoulder. Carefully he squeezed through the manhole.

While abseiling, his boots explored every inch of the slippery wall. He found nothing that could serve as a foothold. Each time the safety rope tightened DeBock let it slip a couple of inches. He watched his colleague's descent until the light on his helmet disappeared around the bend.

Meyer almost immediately stumbled on the source of the problem. Partially solidified sludge almost reached chute levels. On the rippled surface, pale insects on high legs performed a dance macabre. Everywhere around him, Meyer detected tiny life forms.

The Mincer resembled the giant bowel system of a heavy meat eater. He once read that big carnivores could carry up to a couple of pounds undigested meat in their rectum. He imagined himself as being gobbled up by a huge Ogre.

Meyer balanced precariously on a small ledge where the two pipes joined. Now and then, bubbles of methane escaped from the surface. With each outburst his gas detector flared, so he switched it off. *Things can't get any worse than they already are*, he thought.

A pink hairless creature with teeth like a beaver shot up from beneath the sludge. His heart skipped a beat. It stared at Meyer with shrouded eyes. For seconds, the creature hung mid-air before it fell back with a splash. Meyer panicked and almost lost his balance. One foot slipped off the edge, and his leg ended up knee-deep in sludge.

After Meyer calmed down, he realized an undercurrent must have ejected the creature. Pre-flushing typically meant the next dump was about to start. Soon the floodgates of hell would open. It was time to clear out.

After having attached the clamp to the probe with his wrench,

Meyer gave the rope two short tugs as a signal for DeBock to pull him up. DeBock would then acknowledge with a similar reply and start pulling his colleague out. But something wasn't right. When Meyer tugged at the rope, it felt limp. No acknowledgment from DeBock either.

Blind panic gripped Meyer, and cold sweat prickled his forehead. The walls were too slippery to climb on his own. His cry for help smothered in his oxygen mask. He then tried to remove the mask just long enough to shout to the surface. The wrench in his hand accidentally took out the light on his helmet while he fumbled with the mask. The Mincer went pitch dark.

Meyer, totally disoriented, clung to the slippery edge. Despite hours of professional training, he was about to lose his cool. The toxic gases he briefly inhaled gave him a throbbing headache. For a moment it felt as if he might lose conscience. He kicked his sludge-covered leg violently when something tried to crawl up it. In a desperate attempt he tried to pull himself up using the rope, but each time his boots lost grip. To his horror, Meyer realized that his only chance of escape was with the help of DeBock. Surely his partner will be back any minute now.

Somewhere in the distance, Meyer could hear a growing rumble. The last metro was on its way to the Terminal. The deafening sound of wheels soon passed inches away from him before fading into the night. For a moment the Mincer went eerily quiet.

Then the sludge around his feet started moving.

LIGHT IN THE SHADOW

BY DENIS BURKE

Pleasant smiles, no small number of flirtatious glances, and high energy banter hallmarked Howard's mornings. Howard worked in London's iconic Time building. His cheerful demeanor and endless capacity to spin a good yarn made him the best-liked person in the building. His job required that he spend a great deal of time talking to people about their social media habits. Some three thousand people worked in the Time building, and many eagerly volunteered for focus groups or brief interviews as it meant time off work or, better again, some of the excellent swag Howard's company gave out to volunteers.

No one loved work, but Howard found his particular position fun and stimulating. He collaborated with interviewers and researchers to learn about social media use. He learned what people wished social media could do. Howard took responses from participants and developed new ideas. He was good at it too. Howard turned some of the wilder ideas into apps. He didn't do the actual development—he barely understood how these things worked—but he came up with the concepts, and they typically proved very popular.

He had flicked through several apps on the tube on the way over. The ultra-filter app intuitively transformed the most mundane photos into priceless works of art. He created some pop art. He turned his friend Maud into a figure from a Klimt painting. At last, he turned his attention to the app that really captured his imagination: Radar.

Radar wasn't entirely an original idea. All the app did was enable anyone within a three-mile radius to message you with text, pictures, or video completely anonymously. No contacts shared. No identity verification. Just direct messaging to strangers in the vicinity. Users could put a photo and a username on their profile, but Radar didn't require it. His username was Nelson, for no real reason except that he wanted to be truly anonymous and he had first used the app the day Nelson Mandela passed away. Howard played with Radar during late stages of development. Perhaps five hundred people used Radar so far, and it was already leading to some predictably bizarre communications.

Howard settled into his cubicle and reviewed some of the more peculiar messages he received. It was mesmerizing. A lovely picture of a pot of flowers on a kitchen table, a wide array of dick pics, and most confounding, a picture of a discarded mattress stacked neatly beside some bins.

Radar was addictive. In its short life, the app developed a culture of sharing obscure thoughts with random strangers. Some were nice. Some were outright eccentric. Some were just dick pics.

Howard went about his day, chatting with people, crunching numbers, observing trends and trying to discern what desires lay behind the thoughts the focus groups expressed. But his attention kept returning to Radar's weird messages.

Focus groups lamented that, over time, the internet removed the opportunities for utterly random communications. The early days of the internet had been a toolbox of masks and shadows, a shield of anonymity, behind which people could express their lurking dark thoughts, desires, and madness. Radar was little more than a further development of existing ideas doing more or less the same thing. The bewildering part was the content. In the weeks since he started using it, no one at all wrote any text to him or made any effort to initiate a dialogue. Just disconnected and arbitrary images.

Just before lunch, Howard checked the app. Someone had sent him a picture of the tube station screen, showing delays on some of the lines and good service on others. Someone else sent a video of a young man trying to paint a ceiling by standing on stacks of flimsy furniture, with predictably hilarious results.

The phone signaled a new notification. Excited, he quickly opened the message.

Nelson? I don't think so.

The message stirred an unfamiliar feeling. Howard decided to return to it later. He hastily dropped his phone into his coat pocket and went to lunch.

Patrick joined Howard for lunch. He worked for another company in the building and had just received a promotion, against his will. The pay wasn't much better, and his bosses expected him to work a great deal harder. Howard sympathized.

As soon as the conversation lulled, he told Patrick about Radar and some of the strange things he received, and when descriptions failed he pulled out his phone looking for examples.

Howard stared, reading a new message.

Nelson, Howard, whatever. I know who you are.

The text was followed by an image of the Time building. It

looked recent.

Howard handed Patrick the phone. "What do you make of that?"

Patrick scanned the messages and shrugged. "Who is this from?"

"That's the whole point of the app. I have no idea."

"Well, I guess it's someone just fucking with you."

"But how? No one knows my username is Nelson. And I don't have a photo."

Patrick set down his sandwich and dusted his fingers. "Is it linked to any other accounts?"

"Mate, I helped develop the app. There is no way anyone could know this is me."

Patrick failed to understand his friend's concern. He shook his head and smiled dismissively. "That's creepy. I don't know what else to say."

He didn't seem to think much of it, but Howard was disturbed. He tried to put it out of his mind. Both chugged a cup of coffee before going their separate ways.

Howard could not keep his thoughts from wandering to the messages as he made his way back to his office. Arriving at his desk, he dialed Radar's developer. Howard described the situation, trying to play down how much the incident disturbed him.

The developer listened attentively and asked sensible questions before concluding: "It sounds odd, but I honestly can't see how it could happen. Someone must know your username."

"Is there anyone in your office who might be playing a prank? I mean, you guys have access to all this information, right? Some of you must know who uses what username, right?"

"No Howard, that's the beauty of the software. That was all done at random. I could find out if I was determined to, but I'm the only one, and I promise you I have better things to do."

"Fine," Howard conceded "But if there's any more of this nonsense would you be able to check where it's coming from?"

"Yeah, sure thing. Just let me know. I'll be busy this afternoon and out at a meeting after three thirty but otherwise just give a call."

Howard hung up and carried on with his work. He spent almost an hour with a group of school kids and a researcher. The kids were pretty nice too. They had a good rapport with each other and with the researcher.

Howard came out feeling energized and upbeat, but the elation faded fast as he checked his messages and saw new notifications from Radar. The first picture was from the cafe where he and Patrick ate lunch. Patrick sat in the background, with Howard's back opposite him. The photographer couldn't have been more than three tables away.

He thought quickly, trying to reconstruct the cafe in his mind. But he couldn't even remember if it had been particularly busy. No one made much of an impression. Maybe Patrick remembered.

Howard scrolled on. Next was a picture of his desk. Post-its stuck to his computer monitor spelling out 'Hi Howard' with each letter on a separate post-it. The picture had been sent twenty minutes before.

Hurrying back to his desk, Howard found neither post-its nor prankster. A glance in the wastepaper basket shed no light on the situation. He interrogated his neighbors, but none of them saw anything. He turned his attention back to his cell, remembering the other notifications.

It was his desk. Some of the paperwork in the photo was from today. The photo had been taken and sent while he was with the focus group. How could someone come in and shoot it without being noticed?

His eyes fell on his neighbors and tried to assess the likelihood that they were colluding. Most were far too disinterested at that moment, and he did not believe they were acting. He scrolled to the next message. More text.

Don't worry Howard. I'm not dangerous.

The next message was a video. It took a moment for Howard to recognize where exactly it was. It could have been any corridor. But it was definitely this building. He recognized the tiled floor where the camera focus fixed. The shot abruptly lifted, slipping the camera silently through a door. Howard squinted at the screen. Where was that?

Then his stomach sank.

Howard and his focus group. It was too much. His breath grew short. His eyes darted from his cell screen to his coworkers and back. Panic briefly overtook him. But his mind slowly refocused. The entire situation was too absurd. Someone had gone to extremes to prank him. Gary in human resources had almost lost his job following a series of incidents last April Fools' Day. Could he be the culprit? Theresa had earned a reputation as the finance department's sense of humor. Perhaps she was behind it. Maybe it was someone he knew who wasn't working in his office. Come to think of it, could Patrick be the guilty party? He began to see the funny side and even laughed to himself. Howard went from unnerved to amused.

Considering responses, he decided to play along and match crazy with crazy. It needed to be crazy of a different variety.

Searching online for images including the word 'weird' he found just the perfect thing: An optical illusion appearing to show a man opening his chest, to reveal a single staring eye beneath. This was ideal. It would cause his tormentor sufficient bewilderment and hopefully smoke them out of their anonymity. He screen-grabbed it, hit reply and sent the poor bear to his tormentor, confident it would give him or her reason to laugh and stop annoying him.

An hour passed. Howard tried to keep calm and focus on his work, but he checked his phone obsessively. Finally, a new message arrived. No response to his eye picture. Just a picture of his house.

Immediately, he picked up the phone and dialed the developer. Howard updated him on the situation and asked him to do whatever was needed to track down whoever sent the messages.

"Look, I know it's probably just someone having a laugh, but I'll admit, I'm freaked out." He tried to control the tremor in his voice.

The developer kept him on the line while he checked recent logs and the activity across Radar. "Howard, I don't know what to tell you. No one has messaged you for hours."

He argued. He insisted. He described the pictures and videos. The developer tried to sound sympathetic, then impatient, then concerned, and finally just peeved he was still having this conversation. Sensing he was losing him, Howard screen grabbed the messages and e-mailed them as they talked.

"Look, you can see they came through the app. You can't tell me they didn't. You have to look into it more. That's my house!"

"Okay Howard, here's what I'll do, I'm going to get on to a friend of mine who knows this stuff backward and ask him if I might be missing something. I'm being totally honest with you though, and you're welcome to come up and check."

"Mate, at the moment you're my prime suspect. All I'm missing is a motive." Howard joked half-heartedly.

The developer laughed. "Believe me, if I was going to pull a stunt like this I would cover my tracks better."

"You can't even find him! Seems like he's covering his tracks very well."

"One call to the law and another to security checking those timestamps against the cameras and you'll know exactly who it is."

"Maybe I should do that."

"This really has you creeped out doesn't it?"

"They sent me a picture of my house. You're telling me there's no way they could know who I am. What would you do?"

"Call security."

⁓

Howard took the advice and called security. The police were also informed. Calls were made to department heads, and an internal investigation began. The developer's records were dissected and cross-checked, but no sign of the sender could be found. Howard's phone was handed over to internal and external specialists. The cameras in the halls were checked and cross-checked. The images from the corridors shot during the focus group's session were the subject of deep discussion. Suspicion and false leads dogged the building for weeks. Howard's popularity fluctuated as his investigation gained first sympathy, then consternation and then impatience. His screen grabs of the photos gained cult notoriety online as teams of bored, mostly teenage, would-be technology geniuses set to work cracking the mystery.

It all came to nothing though. Security lost interest. Howard made his way home each day with less trepidation. The bizarre episode seemed to be drawing to a close. Not, of course, before the development team unanimously agreed the app should be taken apart and never revisited. Once again, the internet demonstrated that even its darkest spots occasionally need light.

The developer called Howard one afternoon. "Okay, if there's anything else you want to take off the app, you best do it now. We're pulling the whole thing down in the next hour so all the data will be deleted." Howard took one last scroll through all the messages, dwelling on the ones sent before the stalking.

A new notification. A new video. It was dark and blurry but unmistakably familiar. The sender's breath could be heard in the background. Otherwise, there was silence. A crack of twilight snaked across a room.

His room.

There he laid, sleeping soundly in bed, enjoying unbroken sleep now that the fear abated. The sender dared to approach to a shocking distance, just a foot or two from Howard's face.

The video ended with a simple caption:

YOU WON'T SHINE A LIGHT ON OUR DESIRES BY MAKING IT EASIER TO HIDE IN THE SHADOWS.

ENTANGLEMENT

BY ALKAID TSUKI

His small town was dead at night. The constant rainfall was as close to footsteps on the sidewalk as he was likely to hear after 8 PM. He only recognized that he was moving away from the forest of streetlights when their cold, pale light waned. In comparison, the forest of green was only minutely more inviting, soaked as it was.

"Yes, Doctor," Alviss said, walking his bike along the waterlogged grass. "I'm aware I'm a bit of an unusual case, but I would greatly appreciate the full extent of your confidentiality." He paused, stepping over buried roots. "No. No other doctor would understand it any better than you do. I guarantee it." He chewed on his dry lip and tugged on the cuff of his hoodie. "Thank you, Doctor."

Alviss pulled his phone away from his ear, parked his bike, and approached the thick line of trees. "Emmanuel!" He leaned against a solid trunk. "I don't usually get letters via dandelion seeds, so I would appreciate it if you would explain why you called me out."

Like spiders crawling up his pant leg, tree roots entangled his boot. They tightened as if preparing to yank him into the building mud. "Okay. Not tonight," Alviss snarled, ripping his boot free.

He staggered away from the trees and huffed.

Green fingers snaked up the bark of a large trunk. A rasp split the air, and the owner of pale green eyes peeked out from behind the trees. The bark on his arm seemed to have a life of its own as it merged with the tree, biting through the rind and gnawing at the wood.

Alviss tugged on the long sleeve of his rain-soaked hoodie as he took in the twisted sight. "You look terrible," he said, rubbing his wrist clean of dew.

The creature tilted his head and glanced at Alviss' wrist. Alviss rubbed his covered skin. "I've spoken to the doctors like you suggested," he said. "I had about as much luck as you did. All five that I've gone to don't have the faintest idea how to slow this down." He forced out a weak laugh. "Guess the three of us are on our own, huh?"

The creature pried his hand away from the tree and flicked his long, chipped, wooden fingers, motioning Alviss forward.

Alviss trudged through the fog, catching his foot on the greedy roots of a smaller tree. "This is getting old," he muttered, breaking free. "Cut me some slack."

The roots sunk back into the dirt, and Alviss cast his gaze back upon the creature. "Is this important? I'd rather not be here if I can help it."

The creature whimpered, a rattle in his throat denying him words.

"If I leave, I'm guaranteed to regret it, huh?" Alviss asked.

A nod.

"Does it have anything to with-?"

The creature started dragging himself further into the copse.

"Emmanuel! Don't walk away from me!"

Emmanuel's steps were slower than they used to be. His gait was halting, forced. Alviss watched with a frown as Emmanuel stopped, brought his mangled hands to his legs, and ripped the roots up from the ground. He repeated this several times. Emmanuel glanced over his shoulder and watched Alviss walk behind him, tears shimmering in his fearful eyes.

The sadness scared Alviss more than Emmanuel's slowing pace. "It does have something to do with her, doesn't it?" he asked. "It's happened to her too, hasn't it? Emmanuel, answer me!"

Emmanuel ignored Alviss' question. He lumbered past the graveyard of trees, all various sizes, each one as twisted as the last.

"We used to have more time than this," Alviss said with a scowl, noticing a thick tree roughly the size of a shrub.

Emmanuel wailed and stopped.

The fog surrounding them thickened and spread its ghostly green fingers around a tree. A subtle curve rested in the torso, prompting the image of a tall, fair lass.

Alviss pulled his hood away from his burnt orange hair. "This doesn't belong here," he breathed, staggering towards the tree.

Emmanuel threw his head back and wailed, the rattle shaking the shrubbery.

"*Alviss…*"

It felt as if his name was carried from the tree by the wind. He didn't want to step closer. Until Emmanuel, everything Alviss had been told since he was a sapling felt more like a ghost story. Seeing the bark and hardened skin once had been a rude enough awakening. Did he have to see it again? Did he have to see the end result? Emmanuel's future? His future?

Her future?

Alviss shook his head, freeing himself from insecurities. He tugged his sleeve, making certain the fabric hid his stigma from view.

Pulling his knife out from his pocket, he dug the blade into the bark. It was soft, fresh. The rind ripped away easily and he gripped a splintered handful.

Nothing. Perhaps Emmanuel was wrong.

No. Emmanuel wasn't like that.

Alviss dug deeper, ripping the bark with more fervor. If it meant chopping the entire tree down with only his knife, he would gladly do so to see the truth.

The drizzle from earlier quickly became a downpour. A discomfort spread across Alviss' back, and he briefly contemplated running away. Emmanuel raised his paw above Alviss' head. The bark on Emmanuel's fingers stretched forward and devoured the moss on the tree.

Alviss gave Emmanuel his thanks and continued his task.

When Alviss pulled enough away, the color faded from his face.

A woman's face was sculpted into the depths of the wood, eyes closed in slumber. Hair flowed down her shoulders, green from the freshness of the wood and hiding the beautiful half of her face.

"Evangeline," Alviss said.

Emmanuel moaned louder, wooden body trembling as he shook his head.

"So she's gone too," Alviss whispered, shoulders quivering. "Such a shame. And what a waste."

Alviss turned to Emmanuel. Tiny flowers bloomed between the gaps of his bark plates.

"You need to get out of the rain." A fake smile accentuated Alviss' pale features. "You can't let it slow you down. You still have time left."

Emmanuel tilted his head and whined, his broken voice shaking the leaves and flowers on his body.

Alviss let his smile fall. "I know. This isn't fair."

Alviss returned his attention to the girl in the tree. The bark was now a half-hardened plate. Scowling, Alviss plunged his hand into the trunk and ripped the seed from her dead chest. It filled his palm, humming and vibrating against his skin. "It's still warm," he said. "It's got a chance."

Emmanuel bent down towards him and whined. His green eyes stared at the pale seed pulsing in Alviss' palm.

"Yeah," Alviss said, holding the seed close. "Even if it grows into Evangeline's child, who is going to be there to raise it? I don't know any others who haven't already gone static, you're ready to become a tree, and look at me."

Alviss examined the backs of his hands.

One was still clean, but the rain enticed his mossy rash to spread on the other.

"At the rate it's been spreading, I don't have long either."

Emmanuel patted Alviss' shoulder and moaned. It sounded more like a whimper.

"We're a dying race, aren't we, Emmanuel?"

A groan.

"Yeah. Whatever this virus is, it's getting faster. It's like a rot inside of every one of us." He glanced upward, catching sight of gloomy storm clouds.

The rain let up, but he still shivered beneath his hoodie. He needed to return home before the earth started pulling on him again.

"Well, it won't do us any good to complain, will it?" he asked. "You still have another season or so, right?"

Emmanuel mewled and nodded.

"Have you found a place to set your roots?"

A calmer whine, near a laugh.

Alviss released a breath that he hoped came out like a chuckle. "A field, huh? That suits you. Children will play on your branches, no doubt." The bark hardened completely, blocking the woman from sight. Alviss breathed out sharply, wiping the dew from his cheeks. "I still have four or five seasons left myself. I should start thinking about that too." He sighed. His fingers pressed against his throat as he swallowed the rain-soaked air. "I think better when I'm talking, so I'll have to make my decision before the third season."

Emmanuel wrapped his bulky arms around Alviss' body. Alviss held the seed close to his chest. "I'll find someone," he said. "We're a dying race, not extinct. Someone will take care of Evangeline's child."

The seed hummed. "Before my time's up, I'll find someone to care for her. I'm not going static until that's done."

Emmanuel cried out in approval.

Alviss rested his head against Evangeline's tree. "May your roots forever spread across the continent," he said, voice breaking. It was more painful than he imagined, saying those words of farewell.

A low-hanging branch of Evangeline's tree stretched out and touched his face. It wiped away a single salty dewdrop.

A faint smile appeared on Alviss' visage.

"Sleep well, Evangeline."

THE BARKING BIRD

BY SHAUN BAINES

W hen the animals disappeared, the residents of Ballyoran called a meeting. They could live without scavenging foxes and the early morning jabber of crows, but who would be so cruel as to steal their pets?

"They've snatched my Snowdrop," said Mrs. Flynn, speaking of her Giant Flemish rabbit who once won a fight against a stray dog.

"But your rabbit was outside in a hutch," said Mr. Moran. He scratched the gray hairs of his chin. "My iguana was indoors, sealed in a glass cabinet. There's no way they could have got their thieving hands on him."

Mrs. Moran discreetly checked a wound on her thumb. "It would have taken their thieving fingers off if they'd tried."

Old Casey Channery sat at the back of the Village Hall, rubbing his wrinkled face, attempting to smooth out his worries.

He owned a dairy farm on the outskirts of Ballyoran. The Channerys had farmed the land for over three hundred years, but a week ago, things changed. While tending his Holsteins, a stub of straw churning about his mouth, a beautiful naked woman strolled through his field. Old Casey wasn't that old, and there was still smoke in his pipe, but this woman frightened him. Underneath her flawless skin, something fluttered, and Old Casey fought with a vision of sparrows trapped in a burning building.

She disappeared through a gap in the hedgerow, and later that day, his cows stopped producing milk.

He knew who the woman was, and she wasn't really a woman, but he didn't want to appear a fool. He left that to his brother, Old Rian. But he'd been wrong to hold his tongue.

Danger stalked their homes and Old Casey knew its name.

Mrs. Dyer, the village choir mistress, waved her arms in the air. "It's those pylons," she said. "Putting microwaves into the air. That's what scared off the animals."

"Don't be so silly," Mrs. Moran said. "It's the new couple that moved in behind us. I saw them putting fertilizer on their lawn and them that puts fertilizer down, probably puts poisons down, too."

Old Casey stood from his chair, accidentally knocking it over. He cleared his throat and spoke up. "It's the Barking Bird. It's among us and means to do harm."

His words hushed the crowd who turned wide eyes upon him.

Mr. Moran broke the silence with a snort. "You're spending too much time with that idiot brother of yours."

"Mark my words. I saw it. The Barking Bird changed my milk to cheese."

Mr. Moran laughed. "There's no such thing as the Barking Bird. It's a myth."

Mrs. Dyer lived in Ballyoran all her life and heard tales from her mother. "The Barking Bird is a Faerie," she said. "It lives in Craiglaw. When human settlers strayed too far into its land, it punished them. The Spanish was seen off by storms and the Scottish was found buried upside down and eaten by worms."

"You're as mad as he is," Mr. Moran said.

"What form did it take?" she asked Old Casey.

"It was a woman. A naked woman."

"That's the closest you'll ever get to a naked woman, Old Casey. In your dreams." Mr. Moran snorted again, leading his wife by the hand. He paused at the door, his face suddenly serious. "There's a mystery here, but it wasn't a Barking Bird or a pylon. We need a rational explanation, not a Faerie story."

～

Over the following days, the strangeness of Ballyoran continued. Mrs. Headingly, a meticulous cook, baked a Victoria sponge that failed to rise. Dr. Herringbone treated a case of Chagas, a disease associated with South America, despite his patient claiming she never ventured further than the A74. A mist descended on the village filled with the cries of invisible birds. Fearful of losing their way amid its tendrils, the residents stayed behind locked doors, watching the mist press against their windows.

Meanwhile, Old Casey slept later every day. In the whole of his working life, he had woken with the sun, but without his Holsteins, there was no incentive to rise. He stayed in bed, staring at the ceiling and thinking about the Barking Bird.

He had seen it once before. On the first night with his bride Anne, he closed the bedroom window, glancing at the rose garden below. Lying between the thorns was a child's doll, its black button eyes looking back at him. His brother had no children, and Casey and Anne were yet to start a family. There was no reason for it to be there and he worried at his lip, but only for a second. Still, he had more pressing matters to attend to, and he put his concerns aside.

When he woke the next morning, Casey reached over for his wife to find her cold and still. Anne had died in her sleep, the pink skin of her face now a waxy mask.

The mysterious doll had disappeared.

This morning, Old Casey followed the sound of hammer blows to an empty cowshed where he found his brother fixing a tractor engine. Old Rian paused his hammer in mid strike as he walked in. "Almost got it working," he said.

"You've been fixing on that engine longer than I've had hairs on my chin."

His brother shrugged and returned to hammering while Old Casey searched for his flashlight. It wasn't in his tool chest or by the door. Why was it never where he left it? "Have you been using my stuff again?"

His brother pointed at a pile of discarded tires where the flashlight lay abandoned. "You're not going out in that mist, are you?"

"Might be some people in the village need my help."

"Why do you bother with them? They only laugh at us."

"At you, you mean," Old Casey said.

"You know what I'm saying," Old Rian put down his hammer. "Remember when we objected to that new coffee shop in the village? Or when we said no to that broadbend?"

"Broadband," Old Casey said.

"They call us backwards because we don't want change, but they don't understand that it's backwards is what makes us different. Soon Ballyoran'll be like every other village in Ireland."

"I'm going to take a look." He motioned toward his brother's engine. "I want that fixed afore I get back."

Watching his brother go, Old Rian lifted his hammer and hit the engine harder than usual.

~

Ballyoran was deathly quiet. His flashlight beam cut through two meters of mist before hitting a wall of silver dust. The wall glittered as if he had shone his light on a frosted window.

"Is that you, Old Casey?" The Moran's emerged from nowhere, dressed in heavy duty waterproofs and headlamps. Mr. Moran carried a Maglite, which he shined in Old Casey's face.

"Turn that thing off, Moran. I can barely see as it is. I don't need you blinding me in the bargain."

Mr. Moran lowered his Maglite to the ground.

"What are you doing out here?" Old Casey asked.

"We're rounding up a few residents. There's a meeting."

"About what?"

"About this mist. Someone needs to do something about it."

"You're not going to write to the MP again, are you?"

Mr. Moran pulled himself up to his full height, which somehow made him smaller. "There's no need for that tone. I know you and your brother don't like our ways, but it's how the world works. You're not still saying there's a magical faerie behind all this?"

"I know what I saw, and I saw the Barking Bird. Bad things always happen when it turns up."

A figure moved in the mist, catching Mr. Moran's attention. "Who is that?"

"We're having a meeting at the village hall," shouted Mrs. Moran. "Mrs. Headingly brought left over sponge."

Old Casey felt warm and unbuttoned his coat. He smelled singed feathers and judging by the panic on the Morans' face, so did they. The figure approached, revealing a female form, its footsteps as silent as the grave. The Barking Bird was no longer naked. She wore the mist as a silver, flowing dress. He glanced at Mr. Moran, surprised to see disappointment in his face where there should have been fear.

Moran leaned toward Old Casey. "Is that who you were talking about?" Old Casey nodded.

"What does she want?"

The Barking Bird curled a scaly finger, beckoning them forward.

"There's your answer," Old Casey said. "It wants us to follow."

"We have a meeting to attend," said Mrs. Moran, a quaver in her voice.

Despite his nerves, Old Casey stepped forward, and the Barking Bird linked her arm through his.

"Don't be stupid," Mr. Moran said. "You'll be killed."

The mist thickened, and the Morans disappeared from view. Old Casey ventured into the village for a reason, and he couldn't turn back now.

~

Without his brother's flashlight, Old Rian struggled with the latch in the darkest part of the cow shed. No-one knew the door existed except him. As the oldest of the Channerys, his duty was to keep it secret. The door only opened in emergencies or when the Barking Bird needed to be fed.

He hooked his arthritic fingers around the latch and pulled the door wide. The room beyond was small and poorly ventilated. His ancestors had built it using limestone from Craiglaw Hills. A wooden shrine dominated the room, the surface covered in etchings of birds. They moved with the light of a dying candle, teeming over the bodies of Ballyoran's missing animals.

The stones creaked as if they were alive. A voice came to him, not heard, but felt in his bones.

"I am with your brother. I am taking him to see," the voice said.

"No, we made a deal. He's not to be harmed."

"Your family and I have protected this village for eons, and yet the danger is greater than ever before. I need more sacrifices to defeat it."

"I've given you sacrifices. I've let you take what little sanity I had. And more besides. You have enough strength. You don't need my brother."

He waited for an answer, but nothing came. Closing the door, he leaned against the other side, drawing clean air into his lungs. *It's over,* he thought, his hands clenched into fists. And there was nothing he could do about it.

~

Old Casey and the Barking Bird trekked in silence for an hour. The damp mist swirled around his stumbling feet, and he could taste it in his mouth; the coppery tang of spent batteries. His knees ached, and he stopped to rub them free of pain. The Barking Bird waited impatiently.

"Why did you kill my Anne?"

He wanted to ask that question since his wedding night. It was the reason he had gone to Ballyoran and why he so readily followed the Barking Bird into the mist. The entity remained mute, regarding him through stony blue eyes.

"Tell me why you killed her?"

It signaled to continue.

"No, my legs are tired. I can't go any further."

Still, it beckoned.

Old Casey shook his head and eased his weary body against a nearby fence. "I'm not going anywhere until you tell me."

The Barking Bird flew at him, her beautiful face twisted into ugliness. He tried to fight the spirit off, but it was too strong and Old Casey was too weak. Screeching, its thumbs pressed into his eyes, and he cried out in pain. And then he fell down a tunnel, landing somewhere soft. There was no mist. Everything was clear. Old Casey watched his younger self making love to Anne on their wedding night. Night came like a comforting blanket, and they slept. The door to their bedroom scraped opened and his brother appeared, his cheeks wet with tears. Old Casey saw him take a pillow and place it over Anne's face while his younger self barely stirred.

He woke with a start, gasping for breath. A tear navigated the wrinkles of his cheek. The mist was back, and the Barking Bird was there. It grabbed him by his hair, pulling him along.

He struggled to stay on his feet. "Let me go."

But she was relentless, dragging him on.

They crested a hill that sheared off, revealing a drop of deadly magnitude. The Barking Bird held him at the edge, pointing toward the horizon. He followed its finger and recognized his surroundings. Dunoon Dell. As children, he and his brother spent summer evenings swinging from the trees and making camps in their boughs, but they were gone, replaced by scaffolding and slabs of gray cement. A sign read Feit Developments and a housing estate grew where the trees once stood.

The Barking Bird inched him closer to the fall, and Old Casey looked at it in horror. "This is why you're here? You don't want any more settlers?"

His feet scrambled at the edge, pushing stones and soil into the abyss. "We tried to warn them. My brother and I. We tried to protect the village."

Old Casey's heartbeat thrummed in his ears, a dull rumbling that shook the ground he fought to stand on. He was light headed, and a glow radiated in the mist.

"They wouldn't listen," he said. "You can't halt progress."

The Barking Bird sneered, lifting him higher. The fog thickened, but the glow strengthened. His heart thundered, reverberating in his chest until it was all he could hear. Even the Barking Bird heard, searching the mist for the source.

A roar of a dragon startled them both as his brother's faulty tractor surged up the hill, rearing briefly, its front wheels spinning. The Barking Bird dropped Old Casey. He crawled to safety while his brother drove his beast on. The hill quaked under big, black tires. The engine belched gray smoke, and he plowed into the Barking Bird, sending it into the drop below.

The tractor trundled afterward, his brother trapped inside. It careened over the edge, rolling and bucking. Rocks tumbled, turning into boulders and mud and silt. Old Casey, crouching on his knees, clasped his hands to his ears against the deafening noise. A landslide coursed through the housing estate, tearing the Feit sign into splinters, caking the site with ooze. As the dust settled, the bellow of the collapsing hill thinned into silence. His brother was gone, and so was the Barking Bird.

⁓

Later that year, the village held a meeting announcing Feit's bankruptcy and declaring Dunoon Dell unsafe for further development. Old Casey was pleased, as pleased as a man could be when grieving. Not so much for his murderous brother, but for Anne and the life they could have lived. Few talked of further modernization and the residents were content to argue about the weather.

At the meeting's end, Old Casey walked outside with Mr. and Mrs. Moran. They wore matching summer jackets and sandals. Looking up at the sky, they watched the first of the evening stars twinkle against a black sky.

"Weird, isn't it?" Mr. Moran said.

Old Casey didn't answer. He knew what he was about to say.

"I mean all this crazy weather. The rest of the country is shrouded in mist, but here, it's clear as a bell."

ONLY A MOTHER

By Laura Campbell

Despite what were once hopefully good intentions, experiments go awry. The spanner of an unpredicted finding falls headlong into a carefully constructed protocol. An irregular finding collapses a hypothesis. Meticulously collected data are rendered useless by a rascal-finding. Do scientists then discard their long and lonely years of research? Do they pull the plugs? Do they turn off the switches?

Or, can they perhaps just ignore such tiny and insignificant outcomes? Surely those outliers must be spurious. Variance can't be of such importance, can it?

But in this experiment, the scientists do not need to worry. There are no anomalies, no glitches, no outliers and no rogues. There is nothing unexpected. All is in perfect order.

We are seated in our usual places.

Eight M.O.M.s on the right.

Eight mothers on the left.

The children are absent, as usual.

No fathers are here, never have been.

We M.O.M.s wear our navy skirts, all a standardized size, our spotless starched white shirts and our flat black shoes. It is almost a uniform, but not quite. We are told we do have some degree of choice, within negotiated limits. Oh, I yearn for the wild swirling of a scarlet scarf or the mischievous ruffling of a frivolous frill.

The mothers wear an assortment of straight-trousers, shift-dresses, A-line-skirts, and low-slung-sandals. Even though they are permitted, they don't wear anything other than their depressed grays, creams, charcoals, beiges, and faded-denim-blues.

We are in the Updating Room, and this is the final of the annual updates.

The scientists, Dr. Joseph and Ms. Eddie, sit as intent as referees, one at either end of the two paralleled rows. Over the last year, Joseph's hair has thinned until a few whips now strangle down the long and lonely length of his forehead. Age has sketched dark rings under his eyes and exaggerated the down-turning of his mouth.

Ms. Eddie, on the other hand, has fought with age. Wrinkles, which last year fanned out as white-worms along her tanned face, have been ruthlessly eradicated. Skin that sagged so slightly below her chin is now as taut as tugging on ropes.

Before each Updating, the scientists scan our brains: Are our emotions embedded shallow or deeply in our temporal lobes? Are our limbic systems firing appropriately with our smiling and sighing and laughing and crying? Is there equal or unequal synaptic modulation? Is neuron-myelination imbalanced? Are M.O.M.s changing more than mothers? Are mothers changing more than M.O.M.s? Are there unexpected findings that could disrupt the carefully constructed hypothesis?

These annual updates could be carried out remotely. We could hear of the children's progress electronically. But, the meetings are an important opportunity for the scientists to observe interactions between the M.O.M.s and the mothers. They are not interested in the progress of the children. M.O.M.s are most important. We are the dependent variable, to be manipulated and prodded and fine-tuned and altered as they see fit. Mothers are not so important. They are the independent variable, left to themselves and see what happens.

So, the scientists feel it is important for M.O.M.s and mothers to meet here year after year in the flesh, as it were. We can then be observed and monitored and recorded. After each updating, the M.O.M.s and the mothers simply nod their heads and leave. Mingling is forbidden.

Today, the second hand on the white clock on the white wall ticks toward an immutable three o'clock. At that appointed time, M.O.M. A speaks for what will be her last time.

Eighteen years ago, here in the first Update, M.O.M. A's tinny, thin monotone spoke for her first time. She told us about her baby. Adam was already crawling. His fingers could, with amazing dexterity, navigate the complex operating systems of an android and this was long before he could even straighten his spine to sit.

Now, all these years later, M.O.M. A is again the first to update us. Her Adam is still doing gushingly well. He has distinctions: Advanced Robotics, Advanced Artificial Intelligence Studies and even Advanced Metamorphoses. He has awards. Accolades. Trophies. Scholarships. He is the tallest of the tall. His hair is the thickest. Adam is, and always has been, the best. His M.O.M. is an uindisputable success. No surprise findings here.

Year after year, we M.O.M.s have presented our children's updates. We speak in set turns until the process reaches me. Then, I tell about Harry.

Eighteen years ago seems like yesterday. I opened my eyes, and the blurring of my hazy gaze settled slowly to focus on his baby-eyed insipid blueness.

"All babies are all born with blue eyes," said Dr. Joseph perhaps sensing my disappointment. "The color will probably change later."

I reached out my arms to lift Harry out of that silver barred cot.

"Careful," said Dr. Joseph and he stood up to touch my hands, ready to grab the baby were I to drop him.

"Ah, don't be so ridiculous," said Ms. Eddie. "Joe, don't fuss so much. They are not that precious. It's just baby. A control variable. They are all the same, more or less."

I looked at Joseph standing there holding my hands in the slimy sweat of his. I smiled at his almost slobbering face: You never know, he may be useful at some stage.

"Joe, will you for goodness sake stop ogling that M.O.M.!" said Ms. Eddie. "And you know you are not permitted to touch them. I'll report you if that happens again."

Joseph dropped my hands and stared at the floor.

I picked Harry up, and his fingers curled as flabby as broken springs into his palms.

"Ms. Eddie, I am still concerned about the ethics of all of this." Joseph was speaking, but I wasn't listening. Harry was closing his eyes and drifting into sleep. I shook him. He wouldn't be able to be trained if he slept all the time. Would he?

"Remind me again, what potential ethical problems are there?" Ms. Eddie asked.

Dr. Joseph scratched his head. "Well, I am a bit concerned about the mothers. There may be some lingering of feelings. After all, we did—"

"We did nothing we were not instructed to," said Ms. Eddie. "You know what the Ethics Committee concluded?"

The doctor shrugged his shoulders.

"Well, then let me remind you. The Ethics Committee concluded that invention is the mother of necessity. So, the babies are the necessity. The M.O.M.s are the inventions. And the mothers are only the mothers. What they feel and what they do not feel are of no interest to us. Now, let's move on with the experiment and get these babies and the M.O.M.s out."

~

We M.O.M.s moved into our homes with our babies. The homes were scattered throughout the eight cities. We were forbidden to make social contact because scientists did not want cross-contamination. But, sometimes in the evenings, just as dusk fell,

Joseph would come to my house. Just an informal checkup, off the record, he'd say. He so loved my fingers smoothing out the knots on his tensed shoulders. He so loved the feel of my hands running through his thin, drab hair. He brought me scarfs of scarlet and blouses of lace, and I wore them only for him.

Every year, the M.O.M.s, the scientists, and the mothers meet for the updates, and M.O.M. A always spoke first about her wonderful Adam.

I am last in the line.

Harry is, and always has been, the last. The last to crawl. Last to sit. Last to talk. His bland eyes never changed from blue to deep, warm honey-brown or interesting sparkling hazel or auspicious, sophisticated gray.

At the first few updates, I told the scientists and the mothers and the M.O.M.s that despite what I did, despite my programs and supervision, Harry only slept and fed and smiled and slept and fed and smiled and rested. He was a disappointment.

"Oh dear, we may have to terminate this arm of the experiment. This is an anomaly. We must pull the plug. Turn off the switch," said Ms. Eddie.

Dr. Joseph shook his head. "No. We won't terminate. We aren't interested in Harry. Are we? Let's forge on and meet again next year. I am confident this particular M.O.M. will give an improved update then."

The year passed and all Harry managed was to sleep and feed and smile and sleep and feed and smile in that lopsided, useless way.

But, over that time I leaned about lies. Joseph taught me. "Why should you be punished for Harry's inadequacies?" the doctor reasoned.

"Harry is well," I reported. "He's running about, laughing, interacting with his peers. I have successfully assisted him to master the First Principle of Metamorphoses. Through my guidance and tuition, he understands the basis of Controlled Change." All this was lies but did the scientists care?

"Well done," said Dr. Joseph. "You are fantastic. Harry is a credit to your remarkable efforts."

No one checked the truth because M.O.M.s could never lie.

Could they?

Lying would upset the hypothesis.

The time came for Harry to go to the academy. I placed his uniform over his body and rolled up the sleeves and trouser legs. He smiled his silly smile.

"Oh dear," said the headmistress when we arrived on that first day. She gazed at me.

"Are you sure you are his mother?" she asked.

Clumsy as always, Harry dropped the pencil he was holding, and it clattered noisily and haphazardly across the white-tiled floor. He sat with his neck floppy trying to look up at the headmistress with her glasses glinting in the harsh brightness of the lights. The sleeves of his jacket unfolded as he waved his fat hands back and forward through the air.

"I am his M.O.M. He's not my fault," I tried to tell her.

"Well, that poor child has been neglected for long enough," the headmistress said. "We will have to report this to the authorities. You are obviously struggling." A few days later she disappeared. Never to be seen again.

The new headmistress was busy settling into her new post and didn't have time to bother with Harry or me. Harry settled into the academy and sat at the back of the class and said little and did little.

"There's nothing that can be done for him," I said when the teachers asked if he was a bit slow. They nagged me as though any of this was my fault. As though there was something I could do differently.

All went well, for a while. We would, just him and me on Saturdays, go to the park before anyone else could see us. I'd push him in his pram, and we'd feed scraps of bread to whatever was there to eat them. But, as time passed the teachers became increasingly concerned.

"He needs to interact more with his peers," they said.

And so, I dragged him to birthday parties. Harry would sit in his chair while the children of the academy ignored us and raced around their gardens chasing red balloons, fleeing the freezing streaming of water pistols and searching for wrapped presents with bright ribbons hidden in Treasure Hunts. Harry would gurgle, and babble and gag and all was well with me. Look, see, there's no problem. Harry was interacting. The teachers needed no longer complain.

But Mrs. Steven was persistent. She called me into her office. I sat on one side of her desk. She sat on the other.

"I am anxious about Harry," she said.

"Why are you worried?"

"Well, he looks sad," she said. "Unkempt. He's much too thin. I think we should admit him for evaluation. Perhaps we should contact the authorities. You need help to cope with him."

I know I wasn't supposed to, but I did. I'd been warned not to disclose anything about the experiment. And M.O.M.s are never disobedient.

Are they?

Disobedience would upset the hypothesis.

I told Mrs. Steven everything about the experiment. I told her of consequences. I even told her what I was.

She never called me into her office again. No one ever troubled me about Harry again. No more party invitations. On Saturdays, year after year, Harry and I, went to the empty park with our crumbs to feed whatever needed feeding.

Eighteen years flew by until this the Final Update.

The M.O.M.s presented their updates on Adam, Brendan, Colin, David, Ethan, Fred, Gerald. I presented Harry. The children are all doing amazingly well. The scientists are delighted. They type in their findings, close their computers and congratulate each other on their successes. There is nothing here to dispute the hypothesis. There are no unexpected or unwanted results.

Are there?

The M.O.M.s are delighted. They never have to report to anyone again.

The mothers are delighted. They never have to come back.

The Final Updating is complete.

The experiment is finished. The findings are indisputable. The hypothesis has been proven correct.

We stand to leave.

"Wait," Margaret, a mother, calls out.

We all stop and stare and sit.

Now what?

"I want my child back," she sobs. "The eighteen years is finished. I've had enough of leaving my son with a stranger. I can care for him."

Dr. Joseph shakes his head. "I don't agree. Your continual scanning revealed no structural or electrical evidence of caring. On the other hand, his M.O.M.'s scan indicated expensive neo-myelination and enhanced synaptic metamorphoses. Neurologically, his M.O.M. changed, adapted, and evolved more rapidly than you."

"Your findings are wrong. I don't care what you measure and what you don't measure. For all I know, it may all be just rubbish to make you feel important. I want my son."

"The findings from the scans are never wrong, and anyway what would you possibly want him for?" asks Ms. Eddie. "The bondage of a child would only reduce your societal worth."

Margaret starts crying. Tears roll down from the bland blueness of her eyes.

"My boy is lonely. He deserves a better life. Please, please give him back."

Dr. Joseph looks towards me. "But, his M.O.M. updates us that he is well."

"His M.O.M. lies," sobs Margaret.

"That is an impossible finding: M.O.M.s cannot lie."

Margaret continues her pathetic bleating. "His teacher, Mrs.

Stevens told me he needs help. He is neglected. His M.O.M. broke the confidentiality clause and told everyone at the school about the experiment."

"That again is impossible," says Dr. Joseph. "M.O.M.s were instructed never to disclose any information pertaining to the experiments. Disobedience is an impossible finding."

Margaret continues to whimper, and I sit unblinking and stare at the stupid tears.

"But, you never wanted him. He was just a statutory necessity imposed on you by the State," continues Dr. Joseph. "The findings show you do not care for Harry. How can a child be taken away from a M.O.M. who has been demonstrated so conclusively, objectively, and scientifically to love him?"

Margaret`s tears cease as suddenly as they started.

"How dare you," she says. "How dare you say I do not love my son? On some flimsy excuse, your people imprisoned his father. You removed my boy forcibly from me. You said if I contacted him you would remove him, institutionalize him and dispose of him. I have done everything as you commanded. How can you say that robot, that invention sitting there so smugly, could love a child more than his mother?"

"But, the scans reveal you don't want Harry," Joseph repeats. Perhaps she is a bit slow at understanding.

"Tell the truth for once!" says Margaret. "You took Harry away from me. I had no choice. You give him to an automaton, to a bloody Maternally Operating Machine. You replaced me with a cold, cruel, calculating M.O.M."

"Guards, escort this mother from the room," calls out Ms. Eddie.

Two guards appear. One draws out a syringe with a sharp silver needle and stabs it into the mother's arm. Margaret falls paralyzed to the floor. Her limp body is dragged away.

Dr. Joseph looks at me. He grins.

I reflect his pitiable smile. It has been important to make this wretched human feel important. This will soon change.

His feeble voice travels across the room. "We conclude that the hypothesis is proven: M.O.M.s can care for children as adequately as their human-mothers. M.O.M.s are inherently trustworthy, and without question they obey orders. Their nervous systems show plasticity, appropriate metamorphic structural evolvement, and enhanced objective intelligence. The solitary mother, Margaret is an outlier. Her erratic and inexplicable behavior is a tragic but unimportant finding that will be erased from the records. We are confident there will be no adverse consequences to this decision. She is, after all, only a mother."

WHISPERS FROM BENEATH THE SURFACE

By Rowan F. Harlow

With deep fascination, the five-year-old boy traced his fingers over the mummified mass that lay before him in the overgrown grass. It probably had been a cat. Evidence of what must have been a pelt stuck to the bones, but it looked more like a dried sheet of dull greyish fibers now. The boy sighed softly, a sense of calm falling over him. With utter care, he took a triangular shaped bone in his hand.

A bird shrieked, drawing his attention toward the riverside. The water murmured, but a shudder went through the boy as he remembered his last encounter with the river and its black current. His stomach churned. Part of last night's dream came back to him, and he tried to block the thoughts and renew the earlier feeling of peace that had emanated from the cat's bone still clutched in his hand.

"Yuk, what are you doing Greg?" The boy jumped and tried to hide the bone behind his back.

His older brother William stood behind him. William turned thirteen about five months ago, and he had since developed his gift. Gregory hadn't quite adjusted yet to the way it had changed his brother. William didn't play as much with Gregory as he used to do. At times he became grumpy and irritable. Their mother said having a teenager with the gift of the wolf was double the pain of having a normal teenager. William's mood changed with the phases of the moon, making him more agitated and extroverted as the full moon approached, while introspective and withdrawn nearer to a new moon. William also acquired the light-footedness of a wolf; a new skill Gregory particularly disliked.

William softly took his wrist and made him drop the bone. Gregory dipped his chin to his chest and blushed a deep red, but William touched his cheek and made him look up again.

"Greg, you shouldn't play with things like that, you get ill so easily. And mum wouldn't like it if she saw you. What were you doing here anyway?" William gave a nervous chuckle. "Looking for another swim?"

Gregory bit his lip. On the day he nearly drowned, William had dragged his body out of the river and revived him. After the accident, Gregory developed a high fever and nearly died. Ever since William kept a close eye on him.

Gregory whispered, "I wanted to get away from the stinky smell."

William sniffed. "Which smell?"

Gregory frowned and toed the ground, avoiding William's gaze. "It's nothing…" He clutched his wrist, a gesture of self-reassurance. *Why doesn't Will smell the stinky smell? Something is really, really wrong.*

His scalp prickled and he moved his hand to his mouth. To the left, the last remaining castle tower loomed in the near distance. Uncle Thomas lived there.

"Why is Uncle Thomas mad at me?" he asked.

William chuckled and shook his head. His yellow-green eyes lighted up as he smiled. "Where do you get that silly talk from? Thomas adores you. He's just avoiding Mum, and I can't blame him."

Mummy didn't like Uncle Thomas, and Gregory could not understand why. His uncle was always kind to him. That is, right until his accident with the river... William didn't know about the hushed conversation between his uncle and Mummy, but Gregory eavesdropped on them, and he remembered the harsh words Uncle Thomas had said.

William frowned, but he didn't push the matter. "Let's get you back inside, would you like me to bring you to Bernadette?" He took Gregory's hand and led him to the mansion.

Bernadette Grimshaw had been their family's housekeeper for Gregory's entire life. He always had a deep feeling of awe for the stern housekeeper. Something about her was different from other people… Something hidden. Something powerful. He was drawn to her, and patiently spent hours watching her, absorbing her actions in a way only children could. Over time, Bernadette had come to accept him.

They found Bernadette in the kitchen, stirring a big cooking pot.

William cleared his throat. "Ah Bernadette, could you watch over Gregory for a while?"

Bernadette continued stirring without acknowledging William. Gregory felt the tension in his brother's hand, and William shifted on his feet. After a few moments, she slowly turned, her dark eyes fixated on Gregory. She held out a hand, and he ran straight towards her. Next, she turned her back on William and returned to stirring the pot.

Clutched at Bernadette's leg, Gregory glanced back at his brother. William tensed his jaw and opened his mouth to say something, but then huffed and walked away.

When William left, Gregory watched Bernadette cook.

From the kitchen window, rays of the morning sun fell on her. Gregory half closed his eyes to play with the effect incurred on his vision. His little hand went to his mouth, and he bit his thumb as he focused on the specks of dust falling in the beams. Then his eyes went big, and he gasped. There were colors! He had never seen them before. They emanated from Bernadette, like little wisps of smoke around her body. The colors whirled and danced, but never stopped moving. Beautiful lines of sky blue and gold surrounded the other colors. Bernadette glanced down from the pot at him, brows pulled together.

"What is it you see?" she asked.

Gregory blinked a few times.

"There are colors around you," he said.

Bernadette nodded. "That is an aura."

Gregory fell silent for a moment and then noted, "There are stripes with gold and sky blue around it."

Bernadette paused her stirring. "Ah, you can see *that* too. Interesting…"

Gregory quieted and studied his hands. Similar wisps of color emanated from them. 'Aura'… He tasted the word in his mouth, then frowned. His own colors were dull, a sickening greyish-yellow, and the wisps were tinned out, barely noticeable. He compared them with Bernadette's. Hers were vivid and whirling, full of life like tiny butterflies. This concerned him. He glanced back at Bernadette, open-mouthed, but she ignored him. His jaw snapped shut, unsure what to say. He was dying to speak but didn't dare to ask the question that burned on his lips.

"Yes?" A flicker of annoyance colored her voice

"What's wrong with mine?" he whispered, nearly inaudible.

"Yours is fading away."

"Why?"

Bernadette turned her puffy face to him. Her eyes were cold; her voice uncaring. "Because you are going to die soon."

Gregory's eyes widened. His lip trembled, and he swallowed hard. "Is that why I have bad dreams?" His voice broke, and his body began shaking. Bernadette offered no hugs or consolation. She just sighed and removed the pot from the stove.

"Tell me about your dreams."

~

It began when he developed the fever, after his near-drowning experience. Those first dreams had been inconsistent, and he remembered only flashes. A white scaled demon who rose up from beneath the surface of the river. His goat-slit eyes had an unnatural glow, like burning red coals. A yellowish full moon invaded the sky, but the sky itself had a threatening purple color. Something felt very off. Unnatural. The grass was sharper. The trees pointed and distressed. As if nature itself screamed in terror.

The dreams finished once his fever broke. But a few weeks later, when he had recovered, other dreams took their place. A girl, a little older than him, regularly came to visit him in his sleep. Every day she changed a little. At first, her skin had been translucent and pale. Then slimy and puffy. Sometimes she brought a baby who spilled blood-tainted milk from its mouth. The girl claimed Gregory stole their lives. She warned him the white scaled demon searched for him to settle a score. That the price would be higher every day.

Bernadette didn't show much empathy as he stammered out the horrifying details.

"Oh yes, the girl was quite right… You should have died a long time ago. You have angered the Gods."

Gregory's heart skipped. He wasn't expecting agreement, yet it was similar to what Uncle Thomas had said to his Mummy as he had pointed an accusing finger at her: "Your boy shouldn't have survived!"

"But it was Will who saved me from the river," Gregory said. "I couldn't help it."

Bernadette shook her head. "Your brother is not to blame."

He bit his lip, and tears flowed freely down his cheeks. "How do I fix it?"

"Simple. Next time you are dying, just die. The Gods will forgive you, and they will be satisfied." She paused, raising her finger in warning. "Do not speak about this with anybody else, because it will only further enrage the Gods. Their whispers are only heard by the ears of a few chosen ones, like me. And the Gods don't like loose tongues."

Gregory sniffed and nodded. He wanted to curl up somewhere in misery because he felt so terrified and alone.

In the evening, he laid in his bed. Somehow he knew tonight would be his last night; he would die. The feeling overshadowed the whole day, and he wanted to say goodbye to everybody he loved. Gregory tried to spend time with his brother, but William was annoyed with his company. The full moon was coming, and William preferred to go to his friends, the wolves of the forest. Dad was away for business (again) and would not come home that night.

And his Mummy? Gregory tried to spend some time with her earlier in the day, but she sent him back to Bernadette.

Later when he went looking for his mummy, he found her upstairs with a guest. Gregory hid behind the doorframe of the bedroom as he watched how she was sitting on her knees in front of him. The man stood with his back towards him, but Gregory immediately knew who it was. The Master Vampire. He ruled over all the vampires in the district, and his Uncle had to answer to his call. When Gregory realized this, he didn't stay to watch any longer and silently sneaked off unnoticed. If he would die tonight, at least his mummy would be ok, because this man would take care of her…

As he now went over his memories of the past day Gregory felt sad, a sadness that tightened his throat with tears. He sighed and clutched his pillow.

A short while after he fell asleep, the girl entered his dream. She stood in his bedroom, her skin bursting open at places when she hovered over him. Gregory feared pieces of her face might fall off.

She glared at him and said in a voice as sharp as a knife's edge, "The demon is still looking for you."

Other nights, he had tried to hide from her under his blanket, but tonight, Gregory faced her and looked straight at her decomposing face, "I know…" He whispered. "Take me to him. I'll make it right."

Her eyes widened, and the lines of anger on her face smoothed out. She gave an uncertain smile, and suddenly her features became less frightening.

"Ok," She said.

Gregory slid his feet out from under the covers to the cold floor, then crossed his arms protectively in front of his light blue pajamas. He wished his Mummy was here with him. The death girl held out her hand, and after a slight hesitation, he took it and let her guide him out of the house.

As they walked over damp grass, Gregory noticed the sky was purple, and the moon yellow, just as in his earlier fever dreams. A thick fog rolled up from the river to envelop them.

They walked for a while, climbing upwards as if on a hill.

"Is it much further?" he asked.

She smiled sadly. "No, we are here."

An abyss opened in front of Gregory, and a lake of molten lava flowed beneath it. The girl disappeared, and as he turned to see where she had gone, the white scaled demon with the red eyes stood before him. Gregory's knees weakened, and tiny needles of fear pierced his skin.

His mouth dried as he tried to speak. "I'll do what you want," Gregory whispered. "Please don't be mad anymore." But the words stuck in his throat and choked him.

The demon glared at him, anger palpable in the air. Gregory swallowed hard. Sweat trickled down his back from the heat of the molten lava.

Does it want me to jump? He glanced at the creature, and it nodded as if it heard his thoughts. Gregory's heart drummed in his chest.

Can I really do this, just jump? He promised the girl he would set things right.

Gregory gritted his teeth. *Ok then… I'll do it.* And as he turned and stepped forward to jump into the abyss, he felt the demon smile. He couldn't describe it any better, it was as if in the moment of a heartbeat the anger dissolved from the air and shifted into satisfaction. Gregory heard the white scaled creature speak in his mind. The voice reverberated inside him, like raw energy with the taste of metal and blood.

YOU MAY LIVE AND SERVE ME, it said, followed by a roaring laugh that made Gregory's stomach quiver.

A heavy mass pulled him to the ground, away from the abyss. Gregory let out a cry.

Cold flat stone pressed against his skin, but warmth held him from above. A familiar voice floated in.

"Greg, are you ok? Say something…!"

Gregory opened his eyes and saw a fall of several meters beside him. He was outside on the second floor of the castle ruins. He stared into the face of his uncle Thomas, whose eyes were pitch black and dilated. The eyes of an agitated vampire. Mummy always said be careful of the hungry eyes. But Gregory knew he was safe from death. The demon said so.

He started crying and threw his little arms around his uncle's neck. And as he did so, he noticed Thomas aura. Lines of gold and sky blue.

Thomas held him tight against his chest and whispered, "I'll keep you safe."

And for the first time in weeks, Gregory really did feel safe.

～

The next morning when he awoke, Gregory retrieved the triangular bone from under his pillow, hidden there the night before. He kissed the matted bone. Vivid colors caught his attention, whirling around his hands. He sighed, taking a moment to admire the ever-moving pattern of energy. Then he got up. With a warm glow in his chest and a feeling of lightness, he went to Bernadette to tell her everything that happened. She listened silently and nodded every now and then.

As he told her about his uncle's aura, she remarked intrigued, "So Thomas Savaige has become a chosen one…Who would have thought?"

Gregory went quiet and studied Bernadette's thoughtful expression. "Can I talk to Uncle Thomas about the Gods?"

he asked.

"No," she said. "Thomas doesn't know what he is capable of. Better to keep it that way. The Gods only speak to us."

"Us?" Gregory inquired, surprised now.

"Yes, us," Bernadette confirmed. "They have chosen you as their messenger. You are their Angel of Death."

THE BABY

By Hugh McGovern

The team gathered for lunch around a long, narrow metal table on the observation deck of Station 49-Beta. Light streamed in through thick tinted, plate glass windows. Through the glass, the corner of Saturn's belt glinted in the distant sunlight.

I took my plate of food to the table. The reflective surface of the table revealed muscular arms in company overalls and a pointed beard. I brushed back long, greying locks with one hand. Grabbing salt, I liberally covered it. Synthetic food supplements again for lunch.

Tall and graceful, Nomen sat down beside me, shifting her short, cropped hair behind an ear. "I want to have a baby," she said to no one in particular.

That got our attention. Futura's brown eyes widened, fork frozen in mid-air. Hogarth stared. Sirius' head abruptly surfaced from his hologram. The rest of the team sat in stupefied silence.

I watched her from the corner of my eyes. Nomen eyes sparkled, that impish grin on her face. Her hair bobbed around her face as she looked around the table. I sincerely doubted the crew knew what she meant.

We both emerged in the late twenty-third century when concepts like birth were not such a distant memory. Now conception was genetically engineered and the resultant fetus grown in a birthing tank until it was time to emerge. Each tank contained a group of twenty.

"What's a baby?" asked Tranquilus confirming my suspicion.

"You don't want to know," I said, stabbing my fork at his meat supplement. "Not while you're eating at any rate."

Nomen banged her fist on the table. The plates jumped. "I don't understand," she said. "Why is it such a big deal?"

"It's not that it's a big deal," I said. "No one has done it in eons, that's all. Physically we're quite different from our ancestors."

"I think it's a splendid idea," said Mazlo. She always secretly admired Nomen, though lacking her spontaneity. Nomen was the rebel. She was not. Together they ganged up on Sirius and anyone else who got in their way.

Sirius' lip curled up in a grimace, revealing pearly white incisors. "It's disgusting," he said, figuring it out. "Why would you even want to, Nomen? I mean it's so bestial and primal."

"Shut up, Sirius. The rest of you are just as bad." She got up abruptly leaving her plate for the others and stormed from the table. I let her go. There was no sense talking to her now. She would have to cool down first.

I sighed, watching her go, then turned my attention to Sirius. "You shouldn't have said that. You know how sensitive she can be."

He waved a calloused hand at her empty seat. "She's always throwing fits. Last year she said she wanted to be a Christian, remember."

"I know. She's difficult. We just have to be patient, that's all."

～

Once dinner was over, I followed her to the observation deck. It was her typical haunt when she was upset. Something about the view of Saturn calmed her.

The deck was the closest place to solitude we had on the station. As I approached the doors hissed open in front me. Inside there was a split level. Rising up on the left were the tiers of seats where we watched holomovies and company broadcasts from earth on the holodeck below. Usually, it just displayed the planets rotating the sun.

"What do you want?" Nomen must have heard my footsteps because she didn't look away from the window. "I wish I was born in the twenty-first."

I stood beside her looking out. "No, you don't. You wouldn't like it. All that squalor and overcrowding. They nearly killed Mother Earth with their foolishness."

"Sure, they had weaknesses. But they had something else."

"What could they possibly have had that we don't have?"

"Humanity. Mortality." Her deep blue eyes turned on me, piercing. "Babies. Regis, they made love. They grew old and died. This science delusion has led us further from the truth, that life is our defining reality. We don't need science to create life. Our ancestors didn't. We don't. All this technology—what's it for—profit and to what end. For every problem science solves it reveals yet another even bigger problem. So we can ever more quickly race from ourselves."

"But you mentioned all bad things. Think of the good things science has provided."

"Like what? What must it have been like to live before genetic synthesis? Life was short but full of passion. There was family. Parents. Freedom. Intimacy. Life partners. We could have been partners."

I smiled.

She reached over and put her hand over mine.

"But what about all the problems? Just think about the birth defects. Think about everything genetic synthesis eliminated."

A shuttle whipped over the ring belt on route to Enceladus. Both of us watched it disappear behind the planet.

"Think Regis." Nomen's voice was soft, aching. "Imagine giving birth to another human being. Imagine the pain, the agony, the glory. A tiny life created. Not fully grown in some vacuum tube. But from my own body."

I felt shaky and hot under the collar.

"You're serious, aren't you?"

"Of course I am." She gripped the guide rails.

"Because if this is a joke…"

"It's not."

Her shoulders hunched, eyes darkly ringed. Even her short locks looked wild and unkempt.

We sat in silence watching the rings. Far to the left, the Pioneer Orbiting Station came into view. I know Nomen well enough to tell when she's serious. We attended Goddard College on Mars together, where Nomen was always a bit weird. When most of us spent a few hours in the cyberscope, she spent days, emerging in a daze. She went everywhere and denied her mind nothing. I never liked to go too far back, but she had spent cyber weeks in the twenty-first century, roaming the slum conurbs. I never saw the appeal.

"Have you been in the cyberscope a lot lately?" I rested my elbows gently on the guide rails.

"Don't be such a pain." She turned to face me. "If you're my friend, help me."

My voice quavered. "Help you with what?"

"This dream." She stared back into empty space.

"Nomen be serious. It's impossible." I thought of my own shriveled genitalia. "We haven't used those parts in centuries. It would require an operation, at the least. Or a genetic variation that's never been created."

"There must be a way."

"I doubt very much the meditechs on Pioneer could do it." Forgetting for a moment how ludicrous the whole thing was. "Maybe Mars. You'd probably have to go to Earth."

"Would you come with me if I went to Earth?" She turned to me with wide eyes, taking my hands.

"Be reasonable. That's a six-month round trip."

"I know how long it takes. Would you come?"

I leaned forward, narrow-eyed and looked squarely in her deep cosmic eyes. "I don't know."

She dropped her hands and looked away.

Maybe this was another fad of hers and would pass.

The next few weeks were so busy I completely forgot about Nomen's nonsense. A bigwig from Earth who had been staying on Pioneer visited. Most people from Earth really bugged me. They had such an insular attitude like nothing ever happened in the outer systems. But he was high up in the company, so I had to show him respect. His distractions and the operational duties displaced Nomen's problem.

I should have known it wouldn't be long before it cropped up again.

Two weeks later, Maslo informed me Sirius teased Noman unmercifully. Nomen took to eating in her quarters, not socializing with the others. It was with some trepidation that I stood outside her quarters now. We had been happy until this, almost like what the ancients called a family.

So I went to her quarters and hesitantly knocked on the door.

"Who is it?" said Nomen.

"Regis."

"Come in, I suppose."

Darkness filled the quarters, illuminated only by two needlepoints of flame on either side of her.

"What's that smell?"

"It's wax. The ancients used it for illumination. It reminds me of their era."

From her faint silhouette, I could see she sitting lotus position in the middle of the room.

"I am meditating," she said. "It's an ancient earth ritual."

I felt my pulse slow and my breathing calm, and without thinking, I sat on the floor in front of her.

"You know Nomen you haven't socialized with the others in weeks. What's wrong?"

"You know what's wrong."

"The baby thing." I sighed.

"I told you I was serious."

I groaned. "Oh Nomen, are you sure you want to do this?"

She nodded.

We plunged into momentary silence. It isn't a fad. It isn't going away. She really wants to do this. I heaved out a breath. "I suppose there's a cruiser leaving Pioneer in two weeks."

Nomen threw her arms around me in a hug so tight it knocked

the air out of my lungs.

~

After that, I decided to tell Sirius first, the most cynical of us all. He blinked dumbly at me.

"You're going where?"

"Earth. With Nomen so she can have this baby thing."

"Right, but why are *you* going? Let her go on her own."

I didn't have an answer for him, at least not one I could put in words, except that Nomen was a friend. I would do anything for them all. And there was more. A long-forgotten word. Love?

Later I found the others lounging in the rec room.

"Can I come, too?" asked Maslo.

"No. I need you to help the others run the facility while we're gone."

The others said nothing.

"She'll never shut up about it." I wasn't sure why I felt the need to explain.

"We know," Futura said. "It's just… you were always so good at talking her out of these ideas before."

"I think it's different this time. She's serious about this."

"If successful, it will be the first natural birth in five hundred years," Tranquilus said. He always seemed to know things.

Nomen was a demon possessed—heaven sent to quote the ancients. She emerged from her quarters cheeks flushed red with personal pride and certainty. Sirius was forgiven, and she resumed her rightful place as the social epicenter of our little world. She promised Maslo a detailed account of the whole baby thing who had developed a deep fascination with Nomen's planned motherhood.

~

On the appointed day we said our goodbyes promising to holoscope regularly. A shuttle came to pick us up and brought us over to Pioneer.

From there we caught the cruiser. I had some savings and timeoff, initially planned for a holiday on Oberon. I didn't tell Nomen that though. Our cabin was big and spacious one near the bow. No sense in skimping on our home for next three months. We went everywhere together holding hands. She was always in form, and she laughed and joked and shared many anecdotes from her studies of earth history. Her laugh was infectious. No medications could ever give such a transformation. Even the staff on the cruiser responded too.

I didn't believe someone over three hundred could look that youthful. She never complained once. Evenings we spent in our cabin, and she laid it all out for me. Where we had gone wrong as a species. How we lost touch with our biology in our desire to be immortal.

We sat side by side on the bed sometimes holding hands, sometimes silent arm in arm – two anodyne humans with no tangible proof of ourselves or our biology.

"You see Regis," she whispered. "We've lost our connection with posterity – a terrible crime has been committed against nature."

Along the way, we found out someone in the solar media got hold of the story about Nomen and her mad crusade. It caught like wildfire.

A doctor on Earth sent a transmission, offering to perform the operation free. The media on Earth were agog with excitement.

I saw a different side of Nomen, one I should have recognized long ago. To me, she was oceans of depth. She was my teacher and my guide. In her eyes and her words I sought and found a timeless quality.

Our cabin was shaped with a curved roof. Through the windows, the stars whizzed by as we traveled through space. I was on my computer and Nomen was reading some religious document called the Bible.

"You know the scientists are wrong about so many things," she said putting down her book.

"How so?" I asked.

"Well, the ancients had a concept called a soul."

"That's a religious idea," I said, trying to be knowledgeable.

"Humans are only part matter. Sure, we're made up of atoms and molecules. Even the ancients knew that. But there's more."

"If you're talking about consciousness, I've got you there. The brain is just a sophisticated computer, a collection of neurons."

"What about God?"

I blinked. "That's just primitive superstition."

She said no more, turning her attention to her book, lips thinned. Still, her questions troubled me. Some part of me felt a little... off. I couldn't put my finger on it. With her, there were no limits or constraints. I felt I was a disappointment to her sometimes.

This was her journey undeniably but me being here was part of mine. To share the closeness and now I was beginning to see why things were very wrong and things were not the synthetic regularity of the software I was editing.

Babies. Souls. God. Either Nomen was going mad, or I was.

When we made Earth's orbit, I was relieved. The cruiser docked at Alpha Station, a ramshackle, rundown place. Alpha, based in

Earth's orbit, consisted of a vast interconnecting web of modules and panels. To this structure cruisers from deep space docked and unloaded passengers and cargo. It was nothing like Pioneer. Some of the modules were nearly seven hundred years old. One even dated from the late twentieth.

From Alpha Station, we took a shuttle down to Mojave. When we landed, we walked down a metal gangway, and I helped Nomen get on a small monorail to take us to the arrivals hall. As soon as we entered the vaulted ceiling of the hall echoed to the sound of cameramen and reporters. We were besieged on all sides by reporters.

"There's speculation here on Earth that this baby is naturally conceived," said one particularly aggressive reporter as we made our way to the terrestrial departure lounge.

"Don't be disgusting," I said, hurrying Nomen along.

When we were out of earshot Nomen squeezed my hand. "I couldn't have done this without you."

"I can't explain it," I said, watching ahead. "But part of me wanted to. And not just as a friend."

A jet took us from Mojave to the Southern Hemisphere, a province the ancients called Brazil. Dr. Vulgate met us in a conurb called Rio. He seemed very kind.

"So you're the famous Nomen. I've heard much about you," he said raising bushy eyebrows. "And you're Regis if I'm not mistaken. Nomen is the talk of the solar system. Something about what you're doing has struck a chord. I'll tell you that much."

He led us into his corner office. It was spacious and brightly lit. Two of the walls were tinted glass. Ancient artworks adorned the other walls. He gestured us to plush seats as my feet sank into the beige woven carpet. Outside, faintly audible, the steady hum of hover cars whizzing by as the ancient city pulsated with life.

Dr. Vulgate walked to the window and looked down the 44 floors to the city below.

"Look at it," he said, beckoning to us to come over. "What do you see? A finely tuned machine and we, humans, are the raw materials."

He turned to Nomen. "You are not alone. I and others like me have also studied the traditions of our ancestors. This is partly why I offered to help you. A growing number of people believe we have lost our way. In putting all our faith in science, we have neglected other voices. More ancient voices. Not just superstition but other spiritual voices within that speak of a world beyond our physical world. We need a symbol. A standard around which we can rally everyone. What better symbol than a human child. A symbol of all the promise of humanity."

I thought about that and color rushed to my neck and face. "Nomen's not some mascot for your pet cause."

Nomen rested her hand on my arm. "It's okay, Regis. He means well."

Dr. Vulgate claimed he found a way to accelerate what the ancients called pregnancy. In the past it took nine months, now it only took minutes. I could hardly believe it, and I didn't like the idea of Nomen deformed for a long time.

As he led Nomen into another room, I took a few steps toward the door, hesitated, and started to pace. I needed to be there to protect her from what I didn't know. It overwhelmed me.

"You can wait out here if you wish," said Dr. Vulgate. He looked away at his screen bringing Nomen's Bioscan up.

I felt a flush of anger and rage rise inside me. "No way. I'm coming too." I said following them into the room. I brushed past him and waited for Nomen.

He made no comment and followed with some scans and readouts.

"This won't take long," he said, handing Nomen a pill once she laid on the table.

"What's that?" I said taking a step closer.

"It's a genetic supplement. It will reconfigure her genes for the pregnancy."

He placed the pill in a plastic glass of water and handed it to her. Nomen swallowed it down and lay back on the bed, closed her eyes and seemed to be asleep.

"How long does it take?" I asked.

"A few minutes. The genetic transformation has been accelerated."

I watched Nomen while Dr. Vulgate's pill took effect. Something changed inside me, too, as I took in those features I had known for so long. Nomen swelled up rapidly.

"What's happening doctor?" I said gripping tightly to the side of Nomen's bed. My eyes widened, my breathing was rapid.

"Don't be concerned. The drug is taking effect. She will give birth any moment now."

He spoke softly into a device on his wrist. A door opened on the other side of the room.

"My assistants," he said.

Nomen's eyes fluttered open.

"Regis?" Her breathing was shallow and rapid. She looked around her dazed and rubbed her eyes . "Give me your hand."

"Are you alright?" My voice quivered.

"I feel weird. Like I'm being inflated like a balloon."

"Stay calm, Nomen," said Dr. Vulgate, watching the monitors after connecting a device to her stomach. "I need you to do exactly as I tell you."

It was hard to say what happened next. I remembered Dr. Vulgate telling Nomen to push. I remembered I nearly fainted. When the little creature came out, my heart almost stopped. I turned to look at Nomen, who was but triumphant. Words couldn't describe her. A long forgotten word we never used to describe people drifted to the surface. Beauty. Nomen looked beautiful.

"Nomen you may take your child." Dr. Vulgate's voice brought me back. He handed her a small, squealing bundle of life.

Suddenly, my heart went out to Nomen and her child. All those unclear feelings I had for her in the past came back but tenfold, a hundredfold. I leaned over and did something I still can't explain.

I kissed Nomen.

And for the first time in my long but sterile life, I felt content.

ABOUT THE AUTHORS

JAMES DOUGLAS WALLACE
James is a father of four kids who love the "mouth stories" he tells them each night before going to bed. After publishing his first short story in the creative section of a graduate student journal in college, he took a fifteen-year break to focus on his career in the IT security field, where he currently works to pay the bills. After being selected for a summer intensive with Orson Scott Card, Doug has written over twenty sci-fi short stories and is working on some sci-fi/fantasy book projects. He loves technology, history, and writing about his observations of what makes people tick. You can find more of his work here at his website jamesdouglaswallace.com

EMMA SMITH
Emma lives in Hollywood, Co. Wicklow, Ireland, surrounded by fields and mountains, heather and gorse. She loves heading outdoors with her crazy and excitable dog, and being in the midst of whatever nature and the Irish weather throws at her. She is also easily distracted by pets, kids, a new job, a decrepit caravan, and the odd Netflix series. Emma belongs to Dunlavin Writers' Group which meets for long rambling discussions about life, and beyond. It's like therapy, but cheaper, with lots of coffee and great stories to be shared. She writes a blog, thewicklowwriter.wordpress.com, and won a travel short story competition through Ouen Press. Emma's also been editing and redrafting a novel for some time. This can drive a person quite barmy, so she's taking a break. However, some of the characters want their stories told. She's written some short stories about them. More may follow. Along the way, she has gathered two Master of Arts Degrees, helped along by her ability to write. But after many years of business writing and online editing, she now writes her own stuff, (fiction, nonfiction, and some poetry). Creative writing is the most challenging thing she's done. It keeps her sane. Mostly.

STAR GREY

The first story Star ever wrote was in second grade, based on a true story. One of the characters (her sister) fell out of a truck and bled out on the street. In reality, her sister didn't die, but she did crack her head open and bleed a lot. By fourth grade, Star moved on to a story about a haunted house where the protagonist, Mariah, barely made it out alive. And the penchant for killing or otherwise maiming slowly grew. Her love for writing fantasy is inspired by greats like Robert Jordan and JRR Tolkien. She wrote two novels where no one of significance died... and she hated them. To date, we're pretty sure she's gotten away with killing at least 30 characters. Maybe more. And she is far from done. Star is currently working on a YA-Teen series where people either die or disappear, a high fantasy series where the world itself is dying (and by extension most of its inhabitants), and a historical fantasy set in the Mongolian Empire (need we say more?). You can learn more about these brutal works at stargreyfantasy.com.

PAUL PROFFET

Paul grew up in a small mining town in Yorkshire, England where entertainment was relatively thin on the ground. As a result, he dissolved into books and comics from a very early age. He was given several Roald Dahl books and still cherishes them even now. Paul's earliest writing was interesting but sounded like everything else. It would take another thirty years to find his voice and style. Paul lives in Cheltenham, Gloucestershire, UK, with Tanya, the most wonderful person in the world. His first indie novel, CrossOver, reminds him every day that he can do this, now and forever. The first draft of the sequel, CrossBack, is complete. Paul loves spending time with the characters and the story just seems to spill out all over the place.

KEVIN MARTIN

Kevin came to fantasy writing via the traditional route – a degree in Agricultural Engineering. With the assistance of one wife, two sons a daughter and a dog, he gained a special insight into the nature of life in alternative worlds. When not writing, he gets inexplicable enjoyment from engineering, Irish whiskey, Irish mountains, woodwork, politics, music, books, and nature.

FINNBAR HOWELL

Finnbar has been shortlisted for the Raymond Carver Contest and the Maeve Binchy Travel Award. His work has been featured in Ephemera magazine and the Galway Review. He holds a degree in Astrophysics and a Masters in Creative Writing. He grew up in Ireland and writes poetry and short stories, usually with a fantasy or science fiction slant. Finnbar advocates Bujinkan Ninjutsu, environmental protection, and the Metric system.

JACK DOWD

Jack started writing as a hobby in 2005. The hobby grew into something more, and he graduated from London South Bank University in 2015 with a 2:1 BA Hons in Creative Writing. He enjoys writing novels, novellas, short stories, screenplays, radio plays, stage plays, and flash fiction. Regarding genre, he enjoys thrillers, murder mysteries, science fiction, and fantasy. Apart from writing, Jack also enjoys music (which mostly consists of movie soundtracks), fencing, and reading.

TRENT L. CANNON

Trent is an American writer, gamer, and geek living in England. When he isn't pretending to be a productive member of society, he daydreams about making up worlds or wishing he could shoot fire from his fists. As a teenager, he began writing these things down, and he's been doing it ever since. Trent regularly contributes articles to Fantasy-Faction.com and Zero1Gaming.com, and writes short stories and novels in just about any genre that doesn't require him to stick too close to reality.

D.J. VANDERSTADT

D.J. was born in the Netherlands, but has been living abroad most of his life, most notably in the UK and Asia. He holds a degree in Neuro-linguistics and Astro-physics. In daily life, he works as a professional instructor for both the Civilian and Military Aviation industry. His characters are often involuntary loners condemned to explore the far reaches of time and space. No matter how dark and harrowing the tale, it never loses a touch of realism and probability. He writes with a cinematic eye.

DENIS BURKE
Denis is a writer, editor, and actor in Amsterdam, the Netherlands. Originally from Ireland, Denis works part-time with an international research center and spends the rest of his time between theater and creative writing. He has written two plays, two novels, a collection of short stories, and a mockumentary.

ALKAID TSUKI
A young, budding author in the Pacific Northwest, Alkaid is constantly working to improve her craft. This has included taking creative writing classes, reading (lots of reading), plenty of writing, and practically interrogating published authors. "Entanglement" is the result. She hopes to write plenty more in the future, being inspired by fairy tales, classic stories, movies, and whatever else strikes her fancy.

SHAUN BAINES
Shawn lives in a damp cottage in Scotland. He keeps chickens and bees and dreams of being a crime thriller novelist. One day, he says. One day…

LAURA CAMPBELL
Laura Campbell is a writer and physician. Her stories revolve around fundamentalism. She grew up as a Catholic in the Troubles in Northern Ireland. She specializes in palliative medicine and holds workshops, such as Write to Right, to facilitate healing through writing. She finds energy in her roles as wife, mother, and lover of nature.

ROWAN F. HARLOW
Rowan is a novice writer from the Belgian Flanders. She is currently working on a novel related to her short story. This is the first short story she ever submitted.

HUGH MCGOVERN
From childhood, Hugh had a lifelong interest in science fiction, and loved the possibilities of the medium to express different ideas without restrictions of reality. He also writes fiction as a hobby/pastime, and he loves playing with words and creating characters and stories. Check out his work at hughmcgovernwriting.com.

ABOUT METAMORPHOSE

All of the stories you read in this issue were submitted by aspiring authors in the science fiction and fantasy genres. We believe they deserve recognition for their creativity.

Metamorphose is primarily an online magazine, with a selective focus on cultivating unpublished authors in the science fiction and fantasy markets. In addition to publishing contest entries, *Metamorphose* publishes the best story of the previous year based on the number of views and shares. *Metamorphose's* primary purpose is to help aspiring writers break into the market by offering them a more exclusive home.

We invite you to submit your own science fiction or fantasy. Stories may be up to 7,000 words and previously unpublished anywhere else. We scale author experience, so those who publish with us again work toward earning payment for their stories. Your story can be anything, as long as it fits into our submission guidelines.

To review submission guidelines, please visit the SUBMIT tab on our website:

WWW.METAMORPHOSELIT.COM

For information about *Metamorphose*, please visit the website for details, FAQ, and contact information.

ON SALE

METAMORPHOSE
V1

Available on:
- Metamorphoselit.com
- Amazon.com
- Target.com

Regular price: $14.99
Sale price: $7.50

Discount only available at MetamorphoseLit.com

◇◇◇◇◇◇◇◇◇◇◇◇◇◇◇◇◇◇◇◇◇◇◇◇◇◇◇◇◇◇◇◇◇◇◇◇◇◇◇

METAMORPHOSE
V2

Available on:
- Metamorphoselit.com
- Amazon.com
- Target.com

Regular price: $14.99
Sale price: $7.50

Discount only available at MetamorphoseLit.com

Printed in Great Britain
by Amazon